ESSENCE ASUNDER

BY

FEIND GOTTES

HellBound Books Publishing LLC
Houston, TX, USA

A HellBound Books LLC
Publication

www.hellboundbookspublishing.com

Printed in the United States of America

First, I would like to dedicate this book to all the music that inspired me to start writing in the first place.

Second, the list of people who have helped me get to this point is long so if you've ever supported or encouraged me I thank you from the bottom of my cold black heart.

Last, but not least, a special shout out to you, the reader, for without you there is no point to any of this.

Pleasant nightmares.

Also by Feind Gottes

<u>Short Stories</u>

Hell Awaits appears in the anthology Kill For A Copy

Tamed Brute appears in the anthology Flashes of Darkness: Halloween Special 2015

The Bones of Baby Dolls appears in the anthology KIDS: Volume I

<u>Also Available from Hellbound Books</u>:

Coven of Ignorance appearing in Demons, Devils & Denizens of Hell: Volume I

Black Lodge appearing in Demons, Devils & Denizens of Hell: Volume II

Inhuman Nature appearing in The Big Book of Bootleg Horror: Volume IV

<u>Solo Works Available and Coming Soon</u>:

Harvester of Sorrow (a novelette) available at https://freeditorial.com/en/books/harvester-of-sorrow

Piece It All Back Together – Debut Novel coming Fall 2018!

ESSENCE ASUNDER

Chapter 1

D rip.

Drip.

Drip. Drop.

The crimson tide flowed down the cool, dark surface over the edge and dripping all the way down to the floor. It rolled over and around the curved surface until everything was covered in its cold, dark essence. A pool began to form on the floor. It would soon become an ocean to the multi-legged dwellers of this dank, abandoned corner of hell. The body above was still warm, but for how much longer? Surely given the amount of pooled blood, it looked far worse than reality, the prognosis couldn't be very optimistic.

The winged dwellers of the basement were already circling like vultures. They drove occasionally to test the defenses of the body below. There was little to no reaction, a few meager twitches, but nothing more.. The hand below didn't have the strength left to swing, swat, or even flip-flop back and forth. The breath coming from the lips was so weak it wouldn't have rattled a tissue an inch away. The winged army hovered above waited for the end as much as the mind in the body below did the same. The blood continued to drip while the buzzing horde waited patiently to feast then lay the next generation in the carnage.

Slowly the body on the table began to stir: starting with a few foot twitches, then the hands, and finally it began to open its eyes. The lids seemed heavy as if fifty pound plates were holding them down. Dreadfully slow, they began to open. Given the scene that awaited them, perhaps it would have been better if they had just stayed closed... forever.

At first there was nothing but blackness: a blackness so thick he could taste it. Rather than the embrace of light kissing his slowly widening irises, all he could see was black. The darkness of whatever god-awful place he was in seemed to crush him like a monstrous entity when the pain set in. It was a burning white hot flame bringing vibrant color to the dark. Every color of the rainbow flashed in his mind's eye before settling back to white, a white so blinding it had no equal, not even a midday summer sun.

The pain came in suddenly like flicking on a light switch, making his scream stick in his throat and choke him. His jaw widened as if to swallow the very sun itself. His neck strained giving him the appearance of one whose head may explode at any second. Just as it seemed the burst was imminent he remembered...

BREATHE DAMN IT! BREATHE!

He gasped like a fish out of water for several seconds, but trying to breathe through the gag in his mouth wasn't the easiest thing to do. It took him a few moments to figure out he had to breathe in through his nose and out through his mouth. Such a simple thing, really, when you stop and think about it, but trying to do so while in a small dark place and in immense pain was next to impossible. At this point, he didn't know where the pain was coming from, but it seemed to be coming from every nerve in his body. The worst had seemed to pass for the time being. He lay there for a moment just catching his breath as best he could.

Breathe. Try to think. Breathe. How the fuck did I get here? Where the fuck is here? What the fuck is happening? Where the fuck am I? Breathe. Breathe. Oh, holy fuck!!

He tried lifting his arms only to find he was either tied or handcuffed: only able to move a few inches at most. The table he was tied to seemed to be made of wood, though he couldn't be entirely certain. His ankles were tied down tighter than his wrists. There was a strap around both his waist and chest, and his arms were bound tightly on both sides. He was able to lift his head, but doing so caused the pain to ripple through his body at light speed. He stifled another scream just trying to breathe.

Next, he tried to yell or scream out, but it was about as useless as running head first into a brick wall — only managing to send pain rifling down his spine. Any movement at all seemed to send fresh waves of pain up his spine from all over his body. Finally giving up, he laid still for several seconds trying not to move any more than he needed in order to breathe.

Just breathe. Nice and slow. Niiiice and slooooooooow. That's it... Another flash of pain rippled down his spine.

"FUCK!" He screamed through the gag. *Just breathe, Jacob. Just breathe. Get a hold of yourself. You can get out of this. You have got to get out of this! Whatever we have to do. Right now just get a fucking grip on yourself. What's the last thing I remember? Steady just breathe. Remember. Breathe... Breathe. I came home from... from... Where the fuck was I? From... from fucking Sal's Bar! Of course fucking Sal's Bar! I'm always at fucking Sal's Bar as long as it's a day of the week ending in "y" that is.* (He almost chuckled to himself but thought better of it.) *I walked in, sank into my comfy chair and flicked on the boobtube. What was I watching? It was, ummm, Damn it! It was motherfuckin', sonuvabitch... ahhhh. Fuck! What does it even fucking matter what you were watching dipshit? You're fucking chained to a fucking wooden fucking table in who the fuck knows where. Breathe... just breathe.*

Jacob's eyes were beginning to adjust to his surroundings, though the complete and utter blackness had only faded to a thick blanket of dark grey. Jacob doubted he could even see his hand in front of his face if he could lift his hand. His heart began to race as he heard footsteps coming down a set of stairs somewhere behind him. The steps grew louder until they finally hit the bottom. Jacob didn't know what the floor was made of, but the steps of whoever had entered were muffled compared to those on the stairs. He couldn't tell how far behind him the person was; he just hoped it was someone coming to his aide, but of course it wasn't. No angel of mercy was coming.

The hand that caressed Jacob's cheek was cold like death. Jacob did his best to call out, but it was utterly useless causing daggers of pain to rear their ugly heads again. He couldn't yet see the stranger who had entered, but he was frozen stiff at the thought of whoever was doing this to him. For a second, Jacob thought that blinding, white-hot light of pain had returned again before realizing that an actual light had been switched on. He soon wished it hadn't been. Darkness was better than what he saw. He closed his eyes, but the bright medical light made it impossible to recapture the darkness. No longer able to control himself, a tear trailed from the corner of his eye down his cheek. *What the fuck?! What the fuck am I doing here? I don't deserve this. I don't deserve this!* He had begun to speak aloud, or as loud as his gag would allow.

"Ah owen't e-irv iss! Ah owen't e-irv iss!" Jacob repeated over and over as if it was going to make any difference at all. The only difference his muffled screams made was the immense pain shooting up and down his spine. He knew whoever had done this wasn't going to succumb to the incoherent pleas of a dead man but he couldn't help himself.

The figure loomed behind Jacob just far enough back so that Jacob couldn't see him. The man smiled beneath his surgical mask seeing the terror in Jacob's eyes. He understood fully what Jacob was trying to say, making him smile even broader. He enjoyed the suffering. He found it delightful to see all that fear-made flesh. He loved bringing it out in them. He liked the way it smelled, the way he could taste it in the air. The fear was so palpable, he could feel it clinging to him like a second skin. *So sickly sweet but such a treat*, he thought.

Jacob knew there were tears flowing down his cheeks; worries about his masculinity didn't really seem to hold any weight down here. He had no idea what was happening, but he feared it was only going to get worse. As if awakening strapped to a table in the dark wasn't bad enough by itself, there was the pain that rippled through him with every strain and struggle. There was the trepidation that it was actually going to get worse, that this was as good as it was going to get for the foreseeable future. Jacob wasn't a religious man prone to throwing out prayers to god, but he did so now like anyone would finding themselves in such a position. *Please just get me out of this. Please just get me out of this. I know I haven't exactly been a saint but... Fuck, I haven't been a fucking demon either! If you're up there for fuck's sake just get me the fuck out of here! I wanna go home!*

Jacob knew his pleas were falling on deaf ears, but what the hell else was there to do when doom has its sights set on you? It's not like you're going to start praying to the sun or moon or something. So, Jacob threw his prayers up to whatever entity there may be out there to save him knowing there was no one to hear him up there or down here.

The figure behind him stopped stroking Jacob's cheek for which he was thankful because it was just damn creepy. It gave Jacob what in another time people called, "the willies". It sent a shiver down his spine, causing a fresh wave of pain shooting back up.

By now, Jacob had figured out that the pain was being caused by something puncturing his back, but he had no idea what it could be. It was impossible for him to determine if he was being electrocuted, punctured, or both; the pain sliced straight to the heart of his spine with any minor twitch. All he knew was that whatever was happening to him wasn't good at all.

Jacob could feel the eyes of the stranger staring down at him through the void. His vision was a blur of blinding, white light from the surgical lamp matching the pain he felt. The light reduced some of the doom Jacob felt when the room was filled with thick black nothingness, but not by much. The dark was doom incarnate; it was alive in the room with him threatening to devour him whole.

Jacob could sense movement, though he couldn't yet see his grim companion. The stranger moved around from behind Jacob to stand to his right side. Jacob could just make out the shade of a figure on the periphery of his vision, but it was a blur like a ghost. A better word might be 'specter' given the situation; 'ghost' just didn't seem to carry enough weight to Jacob's mind. Jake almost smiled at the word but nothing about his current situation would allow the smirk he felt twitching to come to fruition.

Smile? How the fuck can you smile now? You're just so damn cute! Strapped to a table about to be...

What was he about to be? A victim, certainly, but a victim of what? Torture? Too late that was already happening. Fear in that moment surged through every fiber of Jacob's being.

What was going to happen to him here? What in the fuck are they going to do to me...?

Suddenly, Jake was blinded as he had stupidly opened his eyes for a second. He cringed, causing another bolt of pain to jolt through him. Unthinking, he attempted to lift a hand to shade his eyes, but of course his shackles prevented any real movement. Jake tried opening his eyelids slightly, but the light was like liquid fire on his retinas. Jake held his eyes shut as tightly as he could; the light still blinded him straight through his scrunched-up lids. Then the light moved back slightly, no longer hovering directly over his face. He dared to peak, only to wish he had just kept his damned eyes shut.

Hovering over him was some sort of demented, dirty surgeon. All Jake could see was a dirty surgeon's mask and a dirty green surgeon's head cover with wisps of greasy grey and black hair sticking out here and there like straw from a bale of hay. It was the eyes that scared the holy hell out of him. The pupils were the brightest blue encompassed by jaundiced sclera and bloodshot worse than a pothead who just smoked a pound of weed. Those eyes were pure evil, harbingers of all that was to come.

"Aught ooh aunt?" Jake struggled to ask his captor what he wanted, but dentist room grunts were all he could manage through his gag.

He thought the man behind the dirty surgical mask was smiling, and he was suddenly glad he couldn't see the face beneath it. In Jake's mind, the smile beneath the mask was evil and vile — a Mad Hatter smile. He closed his eyes again trying to escape the image his mind had conjured, yet it would not fade from his mind's eye. He tried thinking of anything else, but what the hell else can you think about when you're painfully strapped to a table at the mercy of the craziest motherfucker you've ever seen?

Fear raced through Jake's veins as he began to break out in a cold sweat. He had no idea what was going to happen to him or what the madman wanted, feeding his fear. The ghostly Mad Hatter smile lingered in his mind as he dared to open his eyes once again.

Dr. Mad Hatter appeared to have been just hovering while waiting patiently for him to reopen his eyes. He stared down at Jake as a starving wolf stalking down its prey. The wave of fear that rode up Jake's spine caused him to shut his eyes again bracing against the pain. He still had no idea what the origin of his pain was — every little movement brought a fresh surge of pain that set his entire body on fire.

Luckily, as Jake dared to open his eyes once again, Dr. Hatter had moved his gaze slightly, no longer staring straight down at him. The relief was temporary but was at least some relief in this nightmare Jake found himself engulfed in. Sensing his victim had once again dared to open his eyes, the mad doctor snapped his gaze back to Jake who nearly soiled himself. Instead, Jake pissed himself, which felt just as wonderful and terrible. He was somehow relieved but still repulsed by the face that stared back at him. Embarrassment was unable to break through the fear that face induced.

Dr. Hatter apparently did not like the piss one bit as he scowled at Jake with just his eyes, still not saying a single word. Jake's tormentor then motioned swiftly with his left hand in a "come hither" gesture, and Jake found he was not alone in this dark pit with the good doctor after all.

A giant with a disfigured face sprang from the corner and headed directly towards Jake, who wished he had remained ignorant to this other presence in his dark prison. The huge mass of inhumanity was easily seven-foot-tall with a face disfigured by either fire or acid until his face had the appearance of either having been dipped in a deep fryer or a vat of sulfuric acid. Its skin was horribly scarred, giving it the appearance of raw hamburger from the chin to the forehead. As the giant approached, all Jake could see was its rage, pure rage. Its eyes were ablaze similar to that of the good doctor only without the relief of the surgical mask to cover the rest of the horror that was its face.

Before Jake could take in the incredible massiveness of the monster, it was on him and unstrapping him from the table. While being slightly relieved to finally be emancipated from his constraints, Jake cringed at the pain he knew was about to shoot through him from every nerve in his body. In one fell swoop, the monster lifted Jake off the table like anyone else might heft a five-pound bag of potatoes — ironically what Jake felt like as the monster heaved him onto its shoulder with as much difficulty.

Jake did not receive the jolt of pain he had braced for, only a great feeling of relief. As the monster swung around, Jake saw the source of his recent pain; he had been strapped down on a bed of nails, screws, and hooks of varying lengths. Jake couldn't be sure, but they looked rusty. It was hard to tell through the flesh and blood hanging from them slightly glistening in the bright light. Usually, stepping on a rusted nail was followed by a shot, but tetanus seemed the least of his worries down here. The hundreds of wounds immediately began to weep blackened, crimson drops coating his back in a blanket of blood.

The giant slammed him down into a chair that felt like cold metal, though he couldn't really tell. It slammed Jake down so hard that Jake's teeth crashed together in bone crunching fashion. A new, brief jolt of pain raced from his ass to jaw. Before Jake could catch his breath, the giant wrapped its huge mitt around his throat, forcing him back into the chair in perfect posture. He could feel the demented doctor strapping his wrists to the chair's arms, then his ankles to the legs. Lastly, Jake felt a leather strap being pulled around his neck, holding his head tight, and he felt a large sharp spike pressing into the back of his neck. The good doctor strapped him just enough to breathe, and the spike was not piercing his skin so far — at least as far as he could tell.

Jake knew the type of device he was strapped to, though he did not know what it was called. He had seen such a device in a James Bond movie, but he could not remember which one or who had been playing Bond in that one. *Pierce Brosnan*, he thought, but couldn't quite remember as though it made any difference in his current situation anyway. He almost laughed at the frivolity of his thoughts, but laughing was not exactly an option right now. Jake did remember that this type of torture chair device had either a wheel or a large screw that was used to tighten the prisoner's head against the neck spike until eventually it severed the spine. Jake tried to take a deep breath to keep that realization at bay, which worked, but only slightly. Though some relief was better than none.

The chair Jake found himself strapped in was commonly known as The Garrote; It had been used as an interrogation and torture device since the days of the

Spanish Inquisition right up through to modern times, mainly in the far east — places like Cambodia. The James Bond film Jake remembered seeing the chair in was indeed a Pierce Brosnan Bond film, *The World Is Not Enough,* which also had the very sexy Halle Berry in it..

As soon as he was fully strapped into the chair, the beast of a man retreated back into his corner, never uttering more than a disgusted grunt in Jake's direction. The good doctor moved around in front of Jake and began his cold evil stare once again.

Dr. Hatter was wearing surgeon's scrubs with a heavy black butcher's apron on top of it. He was shorter than the giant that had lifted Jake but still appeared to be well over six feet tall — maybe somewhere around six and a half feet tall. Dr. Hatter was also very thin, appearing frail to Jake. He had his hands folded behind his back, studying Jake like a butcher might eye a side of beef and deciding where to make the first cut.

The chair was at the foot end of the table of nails which Jake had been strapped to facing its head and the mobile surgical light. There was another long table to his left covered with a sheet. Jake couldn't make out what was under the sheet; there were areas where it was relatively flat and places where it sprang up several feet hiding contraptions that Jake did not truly wish to see. Jake was happy for it to be a mystery, for now, as he tried to hold his imagination from running wild.

Stuffed animals. They're just stuffed animals under that sheet, that's all. You're going to find out this is all just some prank someone is playing on you. Not a very funny prank but just a prank. How can it be anything else? These two are obviously just actors hired by someone to fuck with you. No one actually looks as evil as these two pranksters. That was some really great make-up on the big one over there. That's it, this is all just one big prank, and in a moment they're going to set you free and someone's going to have a big laugh followed by a boot straight up their ass!

Jake nearly smiled, then thought better of it. The last thing he wanted was the gruesome looking doctor smiling back at him again. *What a creepy looking motherfucker this guy was*, Jake thought. The thought of this being some excellent make-up job making the man look like a surgical, car mechanic butcher was perfect. He appeared to be splattered all over with blood, grease, and several other unidentifiable stains that Jake preferred not to think about. The mere thought of what all those stains were, and where they came from, sent a chill up his spine. Thankfully, the chill no longer sent a thousand lightning flashes of pain down his spine, but it was still painful nonetheless.

A true chill shot up Jake's spine as the demented doctor gave him a look of pure evil, slowly turning his head to the covered table where it lingered, tilting slightly like a puppy looking at a shiny new bone. He slowly turned his gaze back to Jake, who could tell the doctor was smiling bigger than ever. For a second, Jake thought he was going to do more than piss himself — Dr. Mad Hatter held his gaze for what seemed an eternity. However, Jake's puckered sphincter held fast saving him another visit from the giant monster in the corner behind him.

Dr. Hatter turned to the head of the table Jake had been strapped to and turned off the light, which Jake observed before everything went black that it was a hospital type examination light. The blackness of the place again engulfed Jake, but he thought he could relax, if only for a moment.

Jake tried wiggling his wrists and ankles to see if there was any give to the leather straps holding him fast. The darkness may have hidden his struggling from the sight of his captors, but he found the straps had no give whatsoever. He was close to spazzing out to see if he could loosen them at all but thought better of wasting his energy, hoping against hope he would have some opportunity for escape at some point. He prayed that would happen before Dr. Hatter removed the sheet from the covered table showing him the horrors that awaited him. Jake couldn't help but stare at the covered table as if it would disappear if he only wished hard enough. That thought was like a weight around his neck, pulling him down choking him and forcing the spike into the back of his neck. Damn, if this fucking chair wasn't one uncomfortable motherfucker, he thought.

Jake could hear a slight scuffling of feet on the hard concrete floor but couldn't tell what direction it was going or coming from in the blackness of this prison — torture chamber, but Jake didn't want to think of it that way… yet. He thought he could feel the giant rise up behind him but couldn't tell if the beast was on the move or just hovering somewhere behind him in the blackness. Then, Jake heard the stairs, which first brought him the crazy doctor, creak He couldn't be sure, but he thought both Dr. Mad Hatter and the giant were exiting his dark cell. Jake was correct; he was now alone in the black with his imagination fueling the fear of what was to come.

Alone in the dark, Jake's thoughts bordered on panic as his fate awaited him on a covered table no more than two feet away. His imagination returned to what might be on that table. There were no lollipops or gumdrops under that sheet. There were no stuffed animals like the ones he had given to his nieces and nephews so many times. No, he knew what lay there covered was pure nastiness; he couldn't even imagine how horrible. He had flashes of sharp, glistening metal in all forms of points and sharp edges. He tried blinking the gruesome thoughts away, but; no other images would come. Jake had nowhere near the knowledge needed to truly imagine the horrors that awaited him under that one long white sheet.

Jake didn't know how long he had been in this dank, dark corner of hell, or how much more he would have to endure. All he could hope was that someone, anyone out in the world was looking for him. Hope was all he had unless the shiny badges he once dreaded came to his rescue. That brought him a modicum of hope. Thankfully, he passed out cold. Dreams of rescue were fleeting while the pain that was coming was assured in his nightmares.

Chapter 2

The sun was too bright to look up for even a second without courting blindness. Wildflowers were everywhere with bees, butterflies, and other random winged creatures bounding from one to the next without a care in the world. Humming birds frolicked here and there, and an overwhelming peace hung over the field like an invisible blanket. At play in the fields of the lord, as those of faith might say. A more serene, picturesque landscape would only be available from a skilled artist's hand. And even then, the skills would need to be considerable. Through the beauty of nature's canvas came a figure embodying that beauty in human form.

Jake held his hand up to shield his eyes from the sun in order to see who it was ambling toward him. He recognized her in an instant. Evangeline had come to join him in this magical setting. She looked at him and smiled, a smile only an angel could duplicate. His heart skipped a beat as he managed to smile back as awkwardly as a prepubescent boy. His stomach instantly filled with butterflies as if the multitudes in this dreamscape had all entered his gut at once.

Evangeline was the love of his life. He loved her from the tip of her dark-haired head to the delightfully polished tips of her toes. An angel incarnates before his very eyes. Every inch of her five-foot-six-inch frame was overflowing with grace and beauty. Perfect curves, perfect smile, utterly perfect to him in every possible way a woman could be perfect. She was humble: lacking the arrogance of a woman who knows she is as stunning as she is. His perfect angel here in this heavenly field on the most beautiful of all days. He thought life just couldn't get any better.

She approached him, the sun at her back framing her in a halo of light as though he could see her very aura surrounding her. The word 'angel' was the only word in his vocabulary that captured what he saw. Her hips swayed ever so slightly, erotically, from side to side as she approached. As she neared, he could see her olive skin glistening as though she had been dipped in honey. A more beautiful vision did not exist in his mind. She wore cut off jean shorts and a bikini top that just screamed 'sexy' inside his brain.

Jake rose to greet the celestial entity before him. He put one hand around her waist and the other on her back, pulling her in tight to him. *She smells like how angels should smell*, he thought, as took her in like a breath of fresh air. He kissed her lightly on the side of the neck where he knew it drove her crazy, in a good way. She leaned back slightly pressing herself into him knowing it's what drove him crazy.

She kissed him lightly on the ear sucking the lobe and whispered, "I love you."

***

SMACK!

The slap was like a shotgun bringing Jake back to life. The deformed giant had decided his captive had rested long enough. The slap shocked Jake to alertness. He lifted his head quickly, driving the sharp spike into the back of his neck. It forced a cry through his pursed lips.

As quick as they'd come, Evangeline and the pristine field were replaced by their polar opposite: the dark basement and at least one of his tormentors. The prison cell, torture chamber, or whatever you wanted to call it was the only reality left to him; the outside world as distant as his dream. There were no sun rays, no butterflies, and no angelic woman to save him from the misery of his present. The giant looming over him was the demon replacing his angel. The bees and butterflies were replaced with centipedes, roaches, and whatever other crawling critters were down here with him. The dream hung in his mind momentarily like a mirage, but it quickly faded as reality smacked him harder than the giant deformity's smack had.

Dr. Mad Hatter was back; he was standing just behind his hideous assistant. Jake swore he could feel the bastard grinning again from behind his dirty surgical mask. He wished he could pound that grin off the doctor's face with his bare fists, but being strapped in the garrote made him feel useless as a rat in a tampon factory. Dr. Hatter circled around his grotesque helper, passing behind Jake, which sent a shiver down his spine. He didn't like the pair standing in front of him, but he really didn't want them behind him or out of sight entirely.

Jake tensed up as he felt the strap around his throat tighten, pressing him hard against the sharp spike at the nape of his neck. Apparently, passing out for a moment meant he had been too comfortable for his tormentors. A feeling of doom washed over Jake like a wave, and hope of rescue died. In that moment, he knew he would never see Evangeline, nor the sun, nor the majestic fields ever again. He came to the realization that he was going to die down here in this dark, musty hell. The only thought filling him was how much pain he was going to have to endure before the end came.

Having tightened the neck strap to the point of agony, the grisly doctor stepped back around the chair to stand in front of Jake again. He tapped the deformed Igor on the shoulder to wave him off. The big galoot frowned at Jake with a look of pure insanity coupled with utter disappointment to see Jake's torment up close. Igor returned to the corner behind Jake but paused a moment looking down at him again with his insane, reddened eyes as if staring at dog shit on his shoe. Without warning, he reared back his right arm smacking Jake open-palmed like a Mike Tyson punch from the former champ's prime. The left side of Jake's face exploded in pain like being hit with a blast of napalm. Igor looked down on him, gave him an evil sneer, then sulked back to his corner until Dr. Mad Hatter summoned him again.

Jake could see the doctor was definitely smiling beneath his grimy surgical mask. Dr. Mad Hatter's eyes seemed to glow with pleasure seeing his victim's pain. Jake could feel the left side of his face swelling up with his left eye squeezing shut from the pressure. Dread filled Jake as he waited for whatever was coming next.

As if hearing Jake's thoughts, Dr. Mad Hatter moved to the corner of the covered table grabbing the sheet covering the horrors that lay beneath. He paused for a moment to revel in the moment. He cocked his head, shot his victim a sinister look, then pulled the sheet slowly and deliberately so Jake wouldn't miss a single horror that awaited him. The doctor didn't pull the sheet completely off, being careful to only show Jake what he wanted to fuel his fear first. All Jake could make out were some odd metal clamps.

Jake could tell the clamps were metal. They appeared to be slightly rusted iron, although Jake suspected some of the rust was actually dried blood; he couldn't be sure. The demented doctor locked on Jake with his jaundiced, bloodshot eyes, staring straight into Jake's soul. Those eyes would haunt Jake forever if he could somehow manage to survive this.

What in the flying fucking Jesus is that motherfucker going to do with that thing? I don't even know what the fuck it is, but I know I ain't gonna like this, not one little bit. Please, for the love of all that's holy let me the fuck out of here! I've endured enough! Just let me go for fuck's sake!

"Ot da uck es dat? Ot da uck!" Jake pleaded, only serving to widen Dr. Mad Hatter's smile from ear to ear.

Slowly and deliberately, the good doctor's wiry hand moved over the metal objects he had revealed on the table. Jake saw that he was correct that the contraption was indeed a clamp, one version amongst many that had been used since the Spanish Inquisition. The clamp Dr. Mad Hatter caressed was a special one that could be used for fingers or toes — able to crush digits individually or all at once depending on the desire of the torturer. The clamp was simple, two thin metal bars with four screws, one for each digit. Each screw was topped by a T-bar handle for ease in applying pressure. Most medieval finger and toe clamps had sharpened teeth along their edges to cut off digits once the clamp was compressed, but this clamp was made to inflict maximum pain, crushing each digit to nothing more that limp meaty oblivion.

Unbeknownst to Jake, Dr. Mad Hatter made all of

his own 'tools' along with giant Igor's help, of course, each designed to inflict maximum pain. Jake didn't know the history of the device, but given the setting, he could guess the use.

Dr. Mad Hatter lifted the clamp from the table moving back directly in front of his victim. He looked from one of Jake's hands to the other, then down at his feet tormenting Jake with the decision of where to begin. He reveled in the trepidation he was creating. A fresh fear sweat broke out over Jake's skin, bringing a wide grin back beneath the dirty surgical mask.

"Uck Ew! Uck Ew, Udderucker!" Jake knew it made no difference but, swearing made him feel slightly better. "Ust et it o'er wit!" Jake's plea to "just get it over with" might have fallen on deaf ears, but to his dismay the creepy doctor seemed to enjoy hearing him beg.

A thick fog of doom hung over Jake, suffocating him like a ton of bricks placed on his chest. His fear so palpable, he could taste it in the air. Jake had hoped that he might somehow make it out of this hell of a basement but seeing the clamp and the pleasure of grim intentions on the doctor's face, he knew his odds were slim to none. Dr. Mad Hatter had only pulled back the sheet on the table a few inches to reveal the clamp, but the table was at least six feet long. Jake looked at the various lumps and bumps of hidden contraptions, increasing his anxiety even further. He had to assume if the doctor had revealed the clamp first, then it was the least of the horrors under that sheet. The thought rattled through his brain as the doctor stood staring down at him with that half unseen mad grin. Jake wasn't sure to be glad for that mask that at least shielded him from the grin or not.

Dr. Mad Hatter was staring Jake straight in the eyes as he motioned Igor to come forward. Jake's stomach flipped at the thought of the big, dumb son of a bitch striking him again. The pain of the giant's smack had mostly subsided, but he imagined the swelling was making him look like the big goon's kin.

Jake felt Igor approach from his corner as the doctor loosened the clamp's screws staring sinisterly down at Jake all the while. A lump formed in Jake's throat, making it hard to breathe. The harder he tried to swallow it away, the worse it seemed to get. Igor was now standing at his left side, waiting for further instruction.

With the clamp open to his satisfaction, Dr. Mad Hatter flicked his eyes to Jake's left hand in apparent direction to his eagerly waiting assistant. The crushing grip of Igor's enormous hands pressed down on Jake's hand, forcing his fingers out straight. Dr. Hatter then slid the clamp over Jake's fingers. He moved slowly with no urgency whatsoever knowing his victim wasn't going anywhere, further fueling Jake's fear. Jake closed his eyes attempting to hide his fear, though it had nowhere to truly hide.

Dr. Mad Hatter slid the clamp all the way to the second knuckle of Jake's fingers. Jake's only relief was that he was right-handed. The thought was fleeting as the doctor began tightening the screws. For the moment, the doctor only tightened the screws enough to create discomfort; Jake knew this was only the beginning. He had learned that his torturer was going to be taking his sweet time savoring every ounce of fear oozing from Jake's pores. The torture had yet to get under way, but Jake's fear could already be tasted in the musty air.

Once the clamp was secured, Igor stayed at Jake's side waiting for more instructions from the doctor and hoping he'd get to watch every torturous second. Dr. Hatter walked back over to the covered table and peeled back the sheet a bit further, revealing three more digit crushing clamps matching the one now secured to Jake's left hand. Dr. Hatter looked down with his back as if contemplating his next move. Then in the most sinister manner, he looked back over his shoulder at Jake. The grin beneath the mask was the widest and most obvious yet.

In the same manner as they had with Jake's left hand, Dr. Mad Hatter and Igor placed clamps on Jake's toes with no haste as his fear rose further. Dread was boiling over in Jake's mind as tears rolled down his cheeks. There was nothing he could do strapped in the garrote chair but watch the horror unfold before his eyes. Even flinching forced the spike, which felt like a broad sword at this point, further into his neck. Jake was smart enough to know remaining still was all he could do to minimize his pain. Fear of what was coming did quell the stinging burn of the puncture wounds in his back, though it was little relief.

After all of his fingers and toes were firmly clamped, the mad doctor motioned for his giant assistant to shuffle off back to his corner which he did with a disappointed grunt. Jake was glad to have the hideously deformed assistant out of sight, though it was little comfort. The good doctor hovered over him still grinning beneath his mask. It seemed he was going to relish every second of torment including the obvious disgust his mere presence caused. The jaundiced bloodshot eyes gave Jake the creeps but that was of little concern when faced with whether he would be forever crippled soon if the doctor ever got down to business. The only real hope remaining for Jake was if the devil before him had any mercy in him at all. Would his fingers and toes be crushed to little meaty sacks forever after to be useless to him, or would his torturer be satisfied inflicting massive pain alone? He could see no mercy in Dr. Mad Hatter's eyes but hoping was the only option his mind had. Without it he'd be consumed by the ever-widening pit of despair his tormentors had opened.

Dr. Hatter stared down at Jake with his arms crossed, grinning for what felt like an eternity —eyeing him up as though unable to decide where to begin inflicting torment. He stared like a child standing in front of a rack of candy trying desperately to decide what to buy with the few bits of change in his pocket. Sweat dripped from Jake's brow as his tormentor finally took a step forward while giving no sign which of his appendages would be crushed out of existence first.

"O uck erelf!" Jake felt a little satisfaction with his slight protest, but the demented doctor didn't seem amused.

Without warning the doctor kicked his leg out nailing Jake squarely in the testicles driving a pain deep into his gut. If there had been anything at all in his stomach, he would have vomited all over the doctor's leg. Jake had doubled his agony by jerking his head back with the kick, forcing the spike deep into his neck — hitting the hard bone of his vertebrae. The excruciating pain in his groin hid the pain from his neck for a moment until he felt blood running down his neck to join the mess on his back. Adding to the agony, Igor broke out in an awful cackle of laughter behind him. A moment later, Dr. Mad Hatter joined his deformed assistant bursting out with an eerie cackle of his own. Anger boiled up in Jake, easing his pain boiling further, knowing he was absolutely helpless; even with his rage, he knew he was going to die down here. He knew it the instant he woke up, but now the thought came home to roost with a will-killing intensity quelling his anger.

Jake lifted his eyes up to his tormentor, shooting the good doctor a look to kill. The look was completely impotent as all three occupants of the basement knew well. Dr. Mad Hatter and Igor were still cackling as Jake felt tears of despair roll from both of his eyes. His dire situation overrode the old adage that "real men don't cry" since it was all he could do.

Dr. Mad Hatter stared, watching as his victim finally began to break in front of him. Jake's tears were manna from heaven to the evil doctor. He waited enjoying the moment before moving in to go to work with the clamps, beginning to cackle again as he did. The doctor took enormous pleasure knowing he was in total control. Adding to Jake's torment, Dr. Mad Hatter began to whistle as though he were just a man out for a stroll on a sunny spring day, rather than the sadistic torturer he was.

Jake felt as useless as a bag of shit. He was already consumed by pain with his prospects getting worse with every passing second. His testicles were aflame, the pain spread from his groin up to his diaphragm, he had nearly paralyzed himself on the spike in his neck, his fingers and toes were about to be crushed to nothing, and sweat was running into the hundreds of puncture wounds in his back feeling like he was under siege from angry hornets. The ball gag in his mouth made it difficult to breathe, but at least it prevented him from giving his two tormentors the satisfaction of hearing him scream like a little girl. Jake began to silently wish for death, though he could see the demented pair were going to make him suffer to his very last breath with no remorse.

The hopelessness of his situation brought new tears to his eyes: tears of anger, frustration, pain and fear. Jake couldn't remember the last time he was afraid of anything in his life, at least not his adult life. As a child, Jake gave himself nightmares with the thought of a witch living in his closet and a tentacled beast hiding under his bed. He had once been so scared of horror movies he could remember hiding under a blanket while his older sister watched *The Exorcist* until he conquered his fear a year or so later, though he still shook with fear the entire time.. Now at 38, Jake was strapped in a garrote chair in a musty, dark basement in god-knows-where being tortured by two goons who looked to have been plucked straight out horror movies that had scared the hell out of him all those years ago. Jake could only sit there trying to breathe through his gag crying and praying for all of this to be one all too real nightmare. He didn't know what he had ever done to deserve this but deep down he knew the answer. It was the same answer in so many of the horror movies he had watched in his youth: nothing.

The basement filled with the thick stench of Jake's fear. Doom hung in the air like dark matter in the universe: unseen but smothering. Dr. Mad Hatter and Igor reveled in it like two children at a birthday party. The doctor hesitated undecidedly as to which digits to crush first. The pair stopped their cackling, but Jake could feel the giant Igor smiling broadly behind him. Jake appreciated the delay in the coming agony, though it did little to nothing to alleviate the fear twisting his gut into knots until finally he couldn't take it anymore.

"Ew etter ucking quill e oz ith I et outa iss I ill quill ew!" Jake threatened with a death stare that only made the doctor grin wider seeing his victim had some fight left in him.

Dr. Mad Hatter leaned forward looking Jake dead in the eye and whispered, "Now I want to hear you scream." Then he removed Jake's gag.

The doctor's first words wiped the bravado from Jake's face as his pupils widened in fear. Dr. Hatter stood to his full height, towering over Jake; he reached up, grabbed his grimy surgical mask, and pulled it down — revealing a demonic grin that would've made Satan himself cringe. He then cocked back his head, crowing like an asylum inmate sending another chill down Jake's spine. Dr. Mad Hatter's smile was a mish-mash of crooked teeth: some sharpened points stained in variations of yellow, brown, and black. It was a vagabond vampire's grin paralyzing Jake with fear as much as it repulsed him. Tears rolled again, seeing that any mercy had left his tormentor many years ago if it had ever existed in the first place.

"Rest assured Jacob, we're going to have us some fun tonight!" Dr. Hatter screeched through the cramped quarters of the basement. The light behind him cast an eerie glow as though hell itself had opened spitting out the heinous hellion.

The doctor's voice was straight out of a horror movie: deep but with a shrieky quality of a baritone hog. The sound alone without any threat brought fresh tears cascading down Jake's cheeks. Jake finally realized that he had no clue what real fear was before this moment; the horror movies of his youth would pale in comparison. He was about to experience a pure evil worse than death up close and personal.

Dr. Mad Hatter relished in turning Jake's face white. He loved the little calm moments before he brought the storm. Questions, followed by threats and defiance, all made the moments sweeter until his weak little victims resigned themselves to the death that never came soon enough. Dr. Hatter savored it like a fine wine tasting every nuance and intricacy of the terror bouquet. He had brought understanding to many, and it never got old. Self-satisfaction fueled his evil grin, but now it was time to have a little fun.

"Left, right, top or bottom?" Dr. Hatter asked.

Jake sat in stunned silence. *Was I actually being asked which digits I wanted crushed to oblivion first? What kind of sick bastard was he dealing with here?* He knew the answer: the sickest he could think of times infinity. Jake bowed his head as much as the neck strap would allow, refusing to answer the freak doctor's question.

"Fingers or toes, my friend?" Dr. Hatter asked again, expecting a reply. "Or would you prefer I make the choice for you? I'll tell you what. If you choose, I'll remove the screws from the others." The good doctor's screechy baritone did not make this choice sound any more appealing. In fact, he sounded like a carnival barker from hell.

Is he really trying to make me choose to lose my fingers or my toes? What kind of sick motherfucker is he? How the fuck can I make a choice like that? Oh, great. It's either I never walk right again or I never use my hands again. Fuck you! You choose, you sick fuck! Then Jake's rational mind kicked in. *If I don't choose, he'll take them all. How can I make a choice like this? I'm going to die down here anyway, so what the fuck difference does it make? All the difference in the world Jake, my boy, all the difference in the world.*

Jake couldn't think any way to decide. He looked up at his tormentor with profound sadness, tears rolling from his eyes hoping to find a shred of mercy there. There was none. The doctor had pulled his mask back up while staring down with his apathetic, jaundiced, bloodshot, insane eyes. There was no mercy to be found in that face. Making matters worse, Dr. Mad Hatter began to tap his foot with the ticking of an invisible clock. Fresh fear sweat broke out over Jake's body returning the salty stings to his back. Jake's only relief was that his testicles had ceased screaming in his gut. The pain settled to a dull ache.

Dr. Mad Hatter then stepped back to the corner of the covered table, grabbing a hold of the corner of the sheet as he had done so meticulously earlier. This time he pulled it all the way back like a magician, revealing the empty box where his beautiful assistant had been only moments before. Jake threw up the only contents of his knotted stomach. Nasty bitter bile filled Jake's mouth and nostrils. The doom he'd felt increased a hundredfold with the display of pain under the sheet. Whatever hope of escape or quick death died in that unveiling.

Dr. Mad Hatter roared with laughter. Igor, who had thankfully been silent back in his little corner of this hell, joined instantly. He sounded like the big, dumb brute while the doctor cackled worse than he had before. Their combined cacophony echoed in Jake's skull long after it ceased. Jake thought his head may burst from the reverberations, but he turned his fear to anger stealing his veins temporarily.

"I will kill you! Mark my words asshole! Mark my words!" Jake's empty threat lacked any power.

Dr. Hatter shot Jake a look of disgust, though it could have been anything. Since his last defiant words had brought him a testicle crushing blow, Jake braced for what he assumed was coming. He closed his eyes to hide from the table of horrors, but no new crushing blow came. Dr. Mad Hatter simply stood there with the light giving an eerie halo again. He stared down at Jake — nothing more than annoying bit of dog shit on his shoe.

Dr. Hatter flicked his head summoning Igor forward. Either the monster wasn't as far behind Jake as he'd thought or he was more spright than he appeared. The doctor took a step back giving the beast more room to do whatever he was going to do. Instead of punching Jake with one of his truck tire sized fists, he just stood there smiling like he was mentally challenged. The gaps in the beast's smile where teeth were missing added to his cartoonish look. He looked like something straight out of a Bugs Bunny cartoon, except that cartoons didn't smell like raw sewage drizzled in garbage similar to the good doctor's breath. The doctor moved forward, dragging the big surgery lamp behind him. He pulled the lamp near Jake's right arm adjusting it to spotlight

Jake's clamped hands and feet.

Dr. Mad Hatter leaned down until his mask tickled Jake's ear. "Choose," The good doctor whispered softly in Jake's ear.

Dr. Mad Hatter reached behind Jake's head with his thin skeletal fingers rubbing the back of his head. He then leaned in until their foreheads lightly touched like lovers about to kiss. If it wasn't for the foul stench emanating from the doctor's lips, Jake would have considered it if it meant getting out of here alive. The doctor was repulsive from a distance, but this close was near unbearable. Jake could see the fucker was still grinning ear to ear awaiting his answer.

"Answer boy!" bellowed the monster towering behind the doctor.

The beast's voice filled the room. It echoed like a shotgun blast in a canyon. A lump grew in Jake's throat preventing an answer he didn't have. His silence seemed to echo as well in the wake of the beast's demand. The air was electric with anticipation as the doctor rubbed his forehead back and forth against Jake's.

"What possible difference does it make? You're going to kill me anyway?" Jake asked with all the contempt he could muster.

At that Dr. Hatter whispered in Jake's ear once again, "The choice before you now is a simple one, choose your fingers, your toes, or both and lose every single one of them. I care not your choice, only that you make one you insolent little cur."

Now that the doctor was so close, Jake could almost taste Dr. Hatter's wretched breath nearly making him gag up bile once again. *Does he eat trucker ass after a week long haul for fuck's sake?* He was only delaying the inevitable choice. He flipped a mental coin. *Heads for fingers and tails for toes*. A fresh, lonely tear streaked down his cheek as he watched the coin flip round and round in his mind until it finally revealed the grim news.

"Left hand, you dirty son of a bitch. Now, will you please tell me why the fuck I'm here? Why me?" Jake hung his head in defeat expecting no answers to his queries.

"Why, you are here because you are stupid mainly, or was it that you're just unlucky?" Dr. Mad Hatter shrugged his shoulders, "Perhaps it was both. Maybe this is all just a case of wrong place, wrong time, my friend, or perhaps it is for something… more. Maybe it was god himself who delivered you to me for a purpose only He knows. It matters not because you, Jacob Falgoust, are fucked." Dr. Mad Hatter's preacher-esque tone assaulted Jake's ear while his sewer breath brought fresh bile to the top of his throat.

Jake mustered what courage he could looking the doctor straight in the eye, "I will kill you for this! Mark my words, I will kill you!"

Igor bellowed out a fresh round of laughter along with the good doctor. He stepped past the doctor, removing the homemade clamps from Jake's feet and right hand. Jake heard them clink as Igor tossed them back on the table. The table that horrified Jake was overflowing with torture devices he didn't recognize. He tried to push the thought of which of those devices would be used on him next by these two psychotics while bracing himself for the pain about to come. Igor stood over him with a mix of immense pleasure and concentration on his face. Sweat dripped from his deformed Cro-Magnon forehead. He was eyeing up Jake like a juicy T-bone steak dinner, just awaiting the doctor's next instructions.

Jake shut his eyes tight, searching for any image to fill his head other than the hulking monster and demented doctor. He searched his mind for his sweet

Evangeline, her beautiful green eyes, her smell of fresh roses, and her smile, but all his fevered brain could find were blood and death. He was near hyperventilation, sitting there with his eyes closed finding only dread in the pain to come. Time had slowed to a crawl, yet nothing happened.

Breathe. Just Breathe Jake. Keep your wits and wait for your moment. They'll get lazy. They'll make a mistake. You'll escape. Any moment, Evangeline will burst through that door with a swat team armed with M-16s to fill these motherfuckers with more holes than Alpine Swiss cheese. Hold on. Breathe.

Doom was a sentient being holding his hand in this hell. It was crushing out the last bits of hope, though Jake desperately struggled to hold on to it. He was riding shotgun with the grim reaper now, waiting to die in this basement. Doom brought the faint scent of death with a wealth of evil Jake had only seen in horror movies, but now he was the star.

"Which first?" Dr. Mad Hatter asked again. The awful stench hit Jake like a ten-ton hammer jolting him back to his reality.

Jake mustered all his will and looked at his foul captor dead in the eye. He uttered slowly and defiantly, "Go fuck yourse—"

Igor's fist landed directly over Jake's rapidly beating heart, stopping it completely for a second. Jake gasped for air, making a horrible noise like an asthmatic suffering his worst attack ever. The Mad Hatter's cackled as though he had just been told the funniest joke ever told.

The psychotic doctor's laughter was contagious; Igor doubled over in laughter, slapping his knee as if he were at a hoedown in hell. While Jake struggled to find his breath, his tormentors reveled in his agony. The blow felt like it had smashed his sternum to dust along with a rib, or four. It took him a minute or two, but he finally caught his breath only to feel unsure if that was in his best interest. All he could do was sit there taking deep breaths while Igor and Dr. Mad Hatter did the same. The blow forced a stream of fresh tears down the dried trails on his cheeks, but they were like an itch that he couldn't scratch as the tears faded. His eyes were bloodshot and burning, his chest felt like an Atomic bomb mushroomed out of it, his back was a bloody stinging mess, and he still had crushed fingers to look forward to along with who knew what else. Prayers for death sprung to his mind again.

Jake heard the 'thwack' before any pain hit him. His eyes shot wide looking down at his left hand where the sound had emanated from. The pain hit him a split second later like the delayed burst of a backdraft. The color drained from his face instantly. His jaw froze unable to even manage a scream as the white hot pain sped up his spine at light speed. He gulped for air, but it was as though his lungs had malfunctioned. He was helpless but to watch as a jet of crimson sprayed out as the doctor unstuck the cleaver from the wooden chair where he had just severed Jake's left pinky finger. The good doctor wiped his hand, adding a new stain to the collection filling his apron, admiring his handiwork.

Jake caught his breath unleashing a scream to wake the dead, "ARGGGGGGGGGGHHHHHH!"

With the nonchalance of Brad Pitt in a singles bar, the good doctor stopped staring at his handiwork leaning in to Jake's ear again speaking with all the kindness of a lover whispering sweet nothings to his betrothed, "Now who's gone and fucked themselves love?"

Jake's head was swimming in pain. He pressed his eyelids together so hard he began to see a kaleidoscope of bright white and red. The images being produced did little to distract his mind from the pain spewing from his hand.

Keep your shit together, man! Breathe. It's only your pinky. It could have been much worse. Keep your shit together man! Breathe damn it! Breathe.

Before Jake could regain any of his composure, Dr. Mad Hatter was back spewing forth his sewage tainted breath again. "You did mean to say left pinky, right?" He was smiling from ear to grimy ear as he asked Jake.

"Just kill me if that's what you want! Just fucking kill me and be done with it!" Jake wanted to sound angry and defiant, but his blubbering sounded instead like that of a pathetic five-year-old begging a bully not to push his face into a pile of shit.

Dr. Mad Hatter stood tall with his hand to his chin pondering Jake's words. He just stood while Jake squirmed and throbbed in pain. Then he slowly, and very calmly, leaned back down until his mask brushed Jake's ear.

"My dear little man, what exactly do you suppose would be the fun in that?" The Mad Hatter whispered his sweet nothings still smiling the devil's grin from ear to ear adding, "We've only just begun, Jacob. You're going to have loads of fun yet."

"Fun? I'm not having any motherfuckin' fun in case you hadn't noticed fuckface! In fact I'm having a downright shitty fuckin' time! Let me go, or just fucking kill me! And again GO FUCK YOURSELF!" Jake had gathered all the courage he could to yell out the words without sounding like a petulant child again.

Did I really just do that? Oh, fuck! It was only a pinky last time. What did I just do? Please, if ever there was a god in heaven, I need your help now. I know I have never given you any credit, but if you're fucking out there I could use a shitload of help right now! Please! If you're really up there you'll help me now! Please! Fuck!

Jake was no believer, but a desperate man will do just about anything. He knew praying would do nothing, but it was all he could do in his current predicament. Either he'd receive some divine intervention, or nothing at all would happen; either way, it couldn't hurt to try. While Jake prayed for salvation, Dr. Mad Hatter stared down at him. He stood there like a wax mannequin from Madame Tussauds museum, seemingly lost in deep thought,   deeper thought than a Buddhist monk meditating. The doctor stood that way for a long moment, allowing Jake to catch his breath to ease the white hot, throbbing pain from his missing pinky finger. Jake's pain was alleviated further when Igor abruptly headed up the stairs, leaving just the doctor with his contemplative stare. Jake took the moment to relax as much as possible and bleed as he waited for the good doctor's next move.

Jake could hear no movement at all from above, which he thought odd since he had lived in several basements and first floor apartments; he knew that even the slightest movement usually sounded like a herd of elephants stomping around, but there was nothing. There were no faint footsteps, no running water, no flushing toilet, absolutely nothing. Jake couldn't for the life of him understand why. Igor looked at least 400 pounds; he should have sounded like a rampaging bull with every step, but there was only silence and Jake's breathing.

"Just where in the fuck are we?" Jake asked Dr. Mad Hatter out of curiosity.

No response came, Dr. Mad Hatter didn't even flinch at Jake's voice in the stillness of the basement. The psycho didn't even glance in his direction, he just stood there statuesque as he had been as though waiting for something. Jake couldn't imagine what he was possibly contemplating, but he was glad for the reprieve no matter how slight it may be.

Jake didn't have to wait long. He had a few minutes of uncomfortable silence with the doctor. Then the door at the top of the stairs opened, giving Jake a brief glimpse of light. Igor was carrying something in his hand, though Jake couldn't make out what it was. The beast moved in slow motion back into the basement. Preoccupied with the deformed giant, Jake nearly missed the doctor give his assistant the slightest of nods. The beast sprang from slow motion to fast forward in the blink of an eye. He shot forward past the doctor to Jake's position, grabbing Jake's left wrist in a vice grip. It was only then that Jake noticed what Igor had brought back with him: a ragged iron bar glowing red at the tip. Jake clenched his teeth bracing for what was coming. Igor brutally shoved the hot tip of the bar to the stub remaining of Jake's pinky.. The pain shot through Jake like a million-amp electrical shock. Then came the smell of searing flesh. He heard the hiss as his flesh sizzled under the iron, forcing bile up his throat once more. He managed to hold it back, though. Igor held the red hot bar to the stump wearing a demented smile. Jake tried desperately not to pass out, but the intense pain from the cauterization was simply too much. Black creeped into Jake's vision as he began to lose conscientiousness.
In one last act of defiance, Jake sat upright looking Igor right in the eye with a look to kill the devil himself, "When you're done burning my hand, don't forget to shove that bar straight up your ass!" Jake spewed. He collapsed into the blissful black unconscious not knowing if he would ever wake up again and hoping he wouldn't.

Chapter 3

Evangeline appeared over Jake like an angel from a Renaissance painting. Her face was love and all that is right in the world. Her dark hair cascaded around his face like gentle waves lapping the shore of a tropical beach. She glowed as if she had floated down from heaven itself. Her skin glistened in the sunshine like that of models he had only seen in magazines, but this was his model; this was his angel. A flood of tranquility enveloped him like a rush of heroin to the brain. He was floating on a cloud in an alternate dimension where the rules of physics no longer applied.

He knew not if he was alive or dead, or if he had awoken in a dream world of his own creation. All Jacob Falgoust knew right now is that Evangeline was with him floating on a cloud of their love. Darkness couldn't enter here. He had his Evangeline, and they were at peace. Their bodies entwined without an Earthly worry to drag them down. Their eyes were locked, each pair peering straight into the soul of the other. In Evangeline's beautiful emerald green eyes, Jake saw the infinite spiral of the universe.. They floated past the moon and past the stars out to the infinite space until they reached the end of all that is known and unknown. They remain blissfully unaware of the cosmic journey as they stared into each other's eyes with lips pressed together as tightly as their bodies. The world fell away as they reached nirvana where nothing existed but their love.

Evangeline was his salvation if he could only hold onto her, but he could already feel their bodies beginning to separate. She was slipping away from him, pulling her lips from his. The separation was tearing him apart, tearing away the very fabric of his being. He was freefalling back through the spiral as his angel hovered above beckoning him to return to her. He felt he was becoming undone, unmade as he fell. He felt himself unraveling as the bliss of pure love turned to the darkness of fear.

The separation was tearing his mind apart. He desperately reached out to rise back up to Evangeline. She held her arms outstretched to him, but he continued to fall away from her. He was falling fast into blackness with his Evangeline fading out of existence. She blew him a kiss with a lonely tear glistening in the corner of her eye, then she was gone leaving only darkness. He was back in the basement, the universe was gone, and love was not allowed here. It had no place. Love suffocated in the dark.

***

The first thing Jake noticed upon regaining consciousness was that he had been moved. He was now lying on a bed. It wasn't the same one he'd woken up to in this place, which had been removed, it was a stinking dirty mattress he found himself on now. The loss of

Evangeline and the feeling of nirvana hung heavy in his mind. He resigned himself to just lie with his eyes closed for as long as he could before his tormentors realized he was awake.

Okay, gather yourself Jake ol' buddy. Keep your breathing under control so they don't realize you're conscious. How in the fuck am I ever going to get out of here? I have to find a way to escape. I gotta get the fuck out of here! Just calm down fuck-o! Breathe. Just breathe. Don't let them know you're awake!

Jake couldn't hear either of his tormentors, the only sound was his own labored breathing. He tried parting his eyelids a tiny fraction to take in his new surroundings but his eyes felt glued shut. *Oh fuck! Did they sew my eyes shut?* Jake tried over and over to part his lids to no avail. He took a deep breath then tried again as hard as he could. Finally after a few agonizing seconds his eyes popped wide open but there was nothing to see but darkness. He thought perhaps he was alone but was unable to discern anything through the blackness, reminding him of being ripped away from Evangeline. A tear gathered at the corner of his eye until finally overflowing rolling slowly down his cheek.

Stop that! She's gone. You're here. Fucking deal with it, asshole! Be grateful she's not here with you so back the fuck up Bucko! Let your eyes adjust and keep an eye out for dumb and dumber. And for fuck's sake, find a damn way out of here!

Jake blinked repeatedly trying to get his eyes to adjust to the gloom. He scanned slowly back and forth trying to catch a glimpse of movement, but there was nothing. He doubted he'd even be able to see his hand in front of his face if he could lift it. He was blind with the creeping taste of death biting at his tongue. He continued to blink, scanning back and forth for what seemed like hours, but there was nothing to see or he was truly blind. He laid his head back in defeat, wiggling his hands and feet to see if there was any hope of slipping his bonds.

As Jake turned his head from side-to-side he noticed that the mattress stunk as bad as Dr. Mad Hatter's breath. It nearly made him vomit bile into his mouth, but he managed to hold it back by holding his breath. *Vomiting now was about the only thing that could make his situation even worse.* He lay there holding his breath as long as he could to keep the horrible stench out of his nostrils. As he did, his mind began to race. His skin began to shiver as if bugs were crawling all over him. Nothing had ever creeped him out more than the feel of a bug crawling across his flesh. If he found an insect on his arm, it was inevitable that he'd feel a thousand more. He wasn't afraid of them, but he'd rather be burned alive than have bugs crawling all over him. Once he let the thought enter his brain, he couldn't shake it. His primal flight response kicked him bringing him to the edge of a full-fledged panic attack. could feel millions of creepy crawlers swarming over him in the dark. He was on the verge of screaming out when it got worse.

"Welcome back friend." Dr. Mad Hatter suddenly whispered into Jake's ear again.

Surprised, Jake couldn't hold back screaming any longer unleashing one loud enough to curdle blood. Jake continued screaming while the doctor stood erect, rearing back in raucous laughter. The doctor's bellows matched Jake's scream, sending an odd cacophony echoing through the confines of the basement. The mixture of screaming and laughter drowned out the sound of Igor returning to the room.

Dr. Mad Hatter was still bellowing as the giant moved beside him. Jake couldn't see the beast, but he knew the fucker was smiling ear to ear. At least he didn't join in with his terrifying howls. Still blind in the dark, Jake couldn't see where either of them was. But from the doctor's laughter, he was standing just behind him. He assumed Igor was right beside him as well.

Dr. Mad Hatter ceased his laughter as abruptly as he had begun, bringing the sweat of feared anticipation back to Jake. Fear had him in a death grip as tight as Igor's meat hook on his wrist while cauterizing him with the hot iron. The sweat rolling off his flesh did nothing to quell his skin crawling from imaginary insects. Jake began to lose control before sobbing lightly.

Light hit him painfully bright as the doctor flicked the surgical lamp back to life. He slammed his eyes shut, but not quickly enough; his head was filled with a bright menagerie of spots. After squinting to see anything in the blackness, the blast of 1000 watt florescence of the lamp blinded him for the opposite reason. His pained expression came as a great joy to his grim captors. Another round of laughter burst out of their decrepit maws. Jake turned his head to the side to escape the blinding glare of the lamp before attempting to open his eyes again, though it took a moment for the fiery ring around his retinas to fade before he could. His mind was still in a fog as the laughter faded and the doctor spoke once again.

"You must be thirsty, no? Hungry?" asked the doctor with the nonchalance of an airline attendant.

Jake was taken back by the question and the doctor's tone. After all he had been through, and all he was yet to experience, the doctor had the gall to speak to him like they were old friends or something.

Jake could only think of one answer and shouted, "Fuck You!" Though, he was as thirsty and hungry as a man lost in the desert for a week.

He had no idea how long he had been down here nor the last thing he had poured down his parched and raw throat, but he couldn't imagine anything the doctor gave him would help. He knew he would probably regret showing defiance once again, but it felt good for the time being. He expected his remark to be greeted with pain, yet punishment was being withheld for the moment. It was only momentary, for if the doctor was to be believed there was no reason he shouldn't be. Jake's lessons in pain had barely begun.

"Well, then we can commence." Dr. Mad Hatter let the final word roll off his tongue slowly accentuated with a hiss.

"Or you and Igor here could just go fuck each other and let me go!" The phrase slipped out of Jake's mouth before he could stop himself knowing immediately that he'd regret it.

What are you doing, you fucking moron? Do you really think provoking these assholes is going to accomplish anything? You can see what's on that table, right? Fuck, you're so stupid! Then again, what is there to lose? These bastards were gonna fuck you up anyway. Maybe if I piss 'em off enough they'll kill me and end it. There's no escape, so what difference does it make? You don't know that. Maybe they'll make a mistake and I can get away. There has to be some way. There just has to be. Be patient and wait for your moment. It'll come. It has to come!

Igor looked to Dr. Mad Hatter seeking approval to afflict brutality, but the doctor stood with a look of profound indifference as if lost in thought. The doctor raised an eyebrow confused to what he should do or if he had heard Jake correctly. The good doctor pursed his lips for a moment at a loss for words then finally relented giving a slight nod to his anxious assistant.

Jake expected Igor to deliver another crushing blow with one of his ham-sized fists, but instead he stepped to the once covered table of torture devices. Dr. Mad

Hatter stared down at him, smiling once again while Igor rummaged through the table like someone rustling through a silverware drawer. The clink and clatter of metal ceased then Igor wheeled a metal cart to the bedside. The cart was too tall for Jake to see what had been laid on it, which he thought was for the best. His heart sank and began to pound vigorously as his imagination ran rampant with what pain was coming his way next.

Fuck, he's gonna cut me open. Please tell me this fucker isn't going to flay me like a fish! Fuck! Fuck! Fuck! Stay calm Jake ol' boy. Stay calm. You're gonna make it, damn it! Just breathe. Just breathe. Panic is the enemy. Breathe.

The reassurances did nothing to stem the fear racing through his veins. Igor had loaded the cart with a gruesome menagerie of surgical equipment: knives, scalpels, picks, and saws most of which Jake had only seen on television. The collection would make a coroner proud except the tools were filthy and rusted bearing the evidence of previous use. There were tools caked with blood, strands of hair, and even bits of flesh left from an untold number of previous victims. The cart various bone saws, skull scrapers, and an ancient and very rusty chest separator. Adrenaline pulsed through Jake's veins at the sight of the only object he could see. Igor had fastened an antique meat grinder to the cart's top like one from a butcher's shop for making hamburger. The silver grinder glistened in the bright florescence of the surgical lamp: the only polished instrument on the cart.

The doctor had a sparkle in his jaundiced eyes as he gazed longingly at the tools. He had his surgical mask pulled down, and Jake thought he looked near drooling from the upturned corners of his grimy mouth. It was the kind of grin that screamed, "I know what I'm about to do and I like it." The look sent a chill down Jake's spine, bringing liquid fire to every single puncture wound on his tattered back, though he barely took notice of the minor stinging. His eyes were locked on the doctor's, fearing what was about to come. He wanted to scream, but he was frozen in panic — choking on it. Time stood still as he waited for the doctor to make a move.

Subconsciously Jake began to squirm as much as his restraints would allow. Tears again began to wash down Jake's cheeks as he lost all hope, succumbing to the fear ripping through him. He stared at the doctor through blurry eyes like an abused dog begging for sympathy that never came. He found no mercy in the doctor's face instead the sinister grin grew to a maniacal rotten toothed sneer. Jake could see that the doctor relished in watching fear consume the helpless victim beneath him. The doctor was a true sadist finding profound pleasure in his victim's agony and the anxiety of agonies to come. Others would call this moment the "calm before the storm," but Dr. Mad Hatter liked to think of it as the "calm before the screaming." The doctor was swimming in an ocean of fear, finding the waters warm like a soothing bath. Dr. Mad Hatter couldn't help basking in the glory of the fear he was squeezing out of every pore on Jacob Falgoust's skin.

"Could I have that drink now?" It was all Jake could think of to break the silence.

The doctor shot back as if Jake had punched him in the face. Unable to stop himself, Jake smirked at the doctor's reaction. He knew he would probably regret that; for the moment, he had thrown the man off his game which was all the satisfaction he could expect. Igor stood slack jawed, seemingly taken aback while waiting patiently for his master's response. He may not know what the doctor would do, but he knew Jake wasn't going to enjoy it which brought a goofy grin to his lips. Igor was the doctor's opposite: relishing in the screams rather than the calm moments between them. Igor longed for the screams of the damned wishing he could play them on an infinite loop. His partner-in-pain had never disappointed him nor their victims.

It only took a moment for the doctor to regain his composure, yet he stood back as though unable to decide his next action. He had witnessed numerous acts of defiance down here, but usually it was nothing more than empty threats speckled with expletives spewed out at him and his large companion. It was the unexpected calmness of Jake's question that had taken him aback. Perhaps Jacob Falgoust was a special case. The thought of breaking him returned the sinister grin to his lips. *This one was going to be fun*, he thought. *Much fun indeed.*

"My apologies Jacob, but I'm afraid that ship has sailed. Perhaps if you wait long enough, it will come back around. While you wait, I think we should have some fun." The doctor's words wiped the grin from Jake's lips completely.

Stay calm. Breathe. You're still alive. You still have a chance to see sweet Evangeline again. Hold her tight, she's all you've got down here.

Jake envisioned his beautiful Evangeline for a fleeting moment. Her dark hair tickled his face as she held him fast with her bright green eyes. It was only a glimpse, but it renewed his will. If beauty could make its way into this hell then perhaps not all hope was lost. He tried desperately to hold the image. His angel lingered in his mind adding steel to his nerves and ebbing the tide of tears flowing from his eyes.

The image vanished completely as the doctor leaned down whispering in his ear once more, "Your suffering hasn't even begun yet, but we'll bathe in your pain momentarily. Oh, what fun I'm going to have with you."

"No, please… why are you doing this? Please, just let me go. Why me?" Jake begged with defeat in his tone. .

Dr. Mad Hatter's lips brushed against Jake's ear. Jake could taste the putrescence spilling from the doctor's open mouth. "Wrong question Jacob. Why not you?" The doctor asked, slowly savoring each word as they slipped from his lips.

"Why not me? Okay, how about because I'm a good person. I've done nothing to you. Nothing to deserve this! Why don't you and Igor there go torture small animals or something? You sick fucks! Go to fucking hell BUT LET ME GO!" Jake yelled in the doctor's face.

"Igor, huh? I kinda like that. What d'you think "Igor"?" The doctor and Igor both chuckled, amused yet unfazed by the suggestion.

The doctor took a deep breath and let out a sarcastic sigh, pausing a moment before leaning back down to Jake's ear to bring his putrid breath. "Dear boy, you do fill my heart with good cheer, but I'm not Dr. Frankenstein and he is not Igor." He then stood up straight as if addressing an audience to proclaim. "I, my dear boy, am Pain and my large friend there is Misery. We are your guides in the darkness. We are destruction made flesh. We have not come here for your body, Jacob. We have come for something much… much sweeter. Do you have a clue what that is?"

"I'm not playing your game asshole!" Jake yelled. "If you want to give a sermon, go to fucking church!" He no longer caring what price would be exacted for his continued defiance.

"Oh, but you are playing Jacob. You are the only piece on the board. Say, I think you just might win!" Pain's words oozed with sarcasm.

"You're out of your fucking mind! No wonder I

thought of you as the Mad Hatter, you're fucking crazy! You need some fucking help, asshole! I know a good therapist, so why don't you let me go and I'll give him a call for you."

"Oh, I'm afraid that didn't work out so well for my last therapist, did it Misery?" Dr. Pain reached down to the cart holding up a surgical saw with blood and hair stuck to the blade. "She did claim to be a head shrinker, and hers certainly did become much, much smaller."

Dr. Pain held up a small saw similar to ones Jake had seen on television but never in real life. The blade was a half circle, maybe three or four inches long attached to an oval handle similar to brass knuckles. Jake thought it was some sort of tool for scrapping brains from a skull which sent another painful chill down his spine. His eyes shot open so wide his eyeballs were about to pop right out of their sockets. Subconsciously, his jaw dropped making him look like a teen on a '50s horror film poster. He tried to bring the image of his sweet Evangeline back in his mind, but he couldn't find her. She was hidden behind a wall of fear built by Pain and Misery — the last people he was likely to ever see.

Tears rolled from his eyes once again, much to the delight of his captors who broke out in a fresh round of laughter. He couldn't figure out why they were taking so much time getting on with killing him, though he was glad for these slight reprieves. He was finding an odd resolve in his pinky's throbbing. The pain was a reminder that he was at least still alive, which meant there could be a chance of making it out, slight as it may be.

Dr. Pain placed the blood and hair caked trepanning saw (its proper name) back on the cart, brushing his hand lightly across the array of instruments like stroking his lover's hair. He looked back and forth from

Jake to his instruments trying to find the perfect match. Dr. Pain then turned back to Jake he with his disgusting gigantic smile again showing off all of his wonderful yellow, brown teeth making Jake cringe.

"Oh, where to begin? Where to begin?" The doctor asked aloud to no one.

Jake stared at him eyes wide and mouth agape with the trepidation of what the demented bastard was about to do. Dread crept over him again. His vision blurred with tears; crying was all he could really do now. The waiting ended in a flash as Dr. Pain abruptly scooped up a rusty scalpel, and with a swing and a flick of his wrist he sliced Jake's abdomen from his floating rib to the belly button. The doctor followed through as if he had taken a perfect golf swing.. The slash was deep enough for the blood to flow. Jake couldn't help but scream.

Before the scream died out and the pain set in, the doctor swung his arm back down without bothering to look and slashed Jake again straight across the abdomen. He crossed the first cut at the navel, making a crude L-shape. The second stroke bit deeper, gushing blood and adding fresh stains to the already filthy mattress. Jake screamed out again as shock and pain hit him like a ton of bricks. The giant, Misery, began his hideous laughter anew.

"No sir. That just won't do at all." Jake was unsure if the doctor was speaking to him or to the scalpel.

Dr. Pain placed the scalpel back on the cart looking vacantly down at his tools. Once again he caressed them lightly back and forth, causing them to clink and clank on the stainless steel tray. There were scalpels of all different sizes, retractors, picks, needles, several homemade devices, and antiques that were more likely to be seen in a medical or torture museum. The doctor was content to let his victim bleed while he quietly pondered what to do next. Misery had stopped laughing, filling the musty air with the weight of silence.

"Stop, please, just stop! You don't have to do this!" Jake pleaded knowing it was futile.

The psychopathic doctor paused for a moment at the plea; his wicked smile returned as he settled on his next instrument of pain. The antique scissors were extremely dull, rusted, stained with crusted blood, and covered with bits of hair stuck in the joint from what Jake could only assume were countless other victims. Dr. Pain couldn't hide his joy as he held up the scissors, opening and closing the blades for Jake to see them clearly.

He moved the cart out of his way to sit down on the edge of the bed. The doctor reached down and wiped away the tears flowing from Jake's eyes as a mother would for her child. He rubbed the tears between his fingers and held them up to the light, staring at them strangely before wiping them across the top of his filthy apron. Dr. Pain caressed Jake's cheek softly again as though attempting to soothe an upset child. For a moment Jake thought of how his mother used to sit by his side when he was sick, doing everything in her power to comfort him. The doctor pulled his surgical mask down slowly revealing his diabolical grin, wiping any thought of his loving mother.

"My apologies Jacob, this could be messy," Dr. Pain said nodding to Misery.

Misery moved with a cat-like silence behind Jake's head. When the doctor nodded, he clamped his hands down on both sides of Jake's head with the crushing strength of an industrial press. Jake yelled, but there was nothing he could do in the monster's grip. He screamed as the grinning beast's face filled his vision.

"Now lay perfectly still, Jacob," The doctor stated, calmly snickering as he opened the scissors.

Dr. Pain slid the blades around Jake's right ear. He pinched them together slowly, watching the fear and pain wash across his helpless victim's face. Jake let loose a blood curdling scream while the doctor pinched the scissors together, one agonizing millimeter at a time. The pure joy in the doctor's jaundiced eyes burned itself on Jake's retinas like the sun at high noon.

"Please! Please! Stop! Please!" Jake screamed to no avail.

The only response he received was another nod from the doctor to his psychotic assistant, but he held the scissors still for a moment. Misery slid his gigantic hands up from the sides of Jake's head so that one was planted firmly on his forehead while the other slammed Jake's mouth shut so hard that Jake nearly bit off the tip of his tongue. Jake's eyes bulged as fear, anger, and pain hit him like a tsunami wave crashing ashore.

The insane surgeon saw all this in his victim's eyes, forcing his smile even wider. With his victim no longer able to annoy him with the usual pleas, the good doctor returned to his slow amputation of Jake's aural protrusion. The blades were as sharp as cardboard; they ripped and pinched as Dr. Pain squeezed the blades together. The maniacal smile on his face was so wide his that cheeks ached, but it only filled the demented surgeon with more joy.

Tears streamed from Jake's eyes as he grunted and squirmed in the monster's concrete grasp. The sick bastard was taking an eternity to amputate his ear, and Jake could feel it being slowly pulled from the side of his head. The scissors were so rusted and dull, the doctor may as well be using pliers to pull it off. As the doctor slowly pinched his right ear off, Misery stared down into Jake's face with all the pleasure his scarred features could muster.

Through his tears Jake could see that the monster's face was a layer of dirt and grime over a patchwork quilt of burnt scars. While some may have taken solace in those scars, possibly where past victims had at least gotten in some damage before dying, Jake saw them for what they were: death in the flesh. The monster had taken some damage, perhaps from other victims in this basement, but since he was still standing it meant that none had been successful. Jake figured that as sick as these two had proven to be, the freak had probably allowed his victims to get in a blow or two just for the fun of it. He saw the pair for what they were… pure sadists.

The monster's eyes were jaundiced and bloodshot just like those of the doctor, adding to his evil more than his hideous face did without them. His long, black greasy hair hung in sweaty strands dripping their ooze disgustingly onto Jake's face. Thankfully, the beast's breath wasn't as bad as the noxious smell emanating from the doctor's mouth, though it was no bouquet of roses.

Jake nearly swallowed his tongue as the doctor finally pinched the blades together with an audible click. The pain burned straight into his brain until he nearly passed out. He managed to hang onto to consciousness, but the pain was almost more than he could bear.. He thought the pain of his finger being cut off was bad, but this was far worse. He found his fear waning, knowing that death was closer now at which point the pain would end. That could be false hope, he knew, since there could be hours or even days of pain left to come. At the moment he preferred to believe death was just around the corner.

"Hello. Hello!" Dr. Pain practically cackled the words holding Jake's severed ear up to his lips, the surgical mask pulled down now as this surgery was over.

The doctor's antic roused a fresh round of laughter from Misery and a look of disgust through the pain of from their patient. Jake doubted he had ever seen anyone happier than the doctor at the moment, not even a mother at the first sight of her child. The thought coupled with pain made him wretch. Burning bile rose to the back of his throat and filled his mouth with its bitter taste while he fought with all his might to keep the vile fluid down.

Dr. Pain admired his fleshy prize for a few moments, flapping it around like a rubber prop before motioning for Misery to come to him. The giant towered over the doctor by more than a foot. The doctor handed his prize to the hulking monstrosity. Jake swore he saw the doctor give the beast another of his little nods through his still blurry vision.

The beast turned to face Jake, looked him straight in the eyes and gave him one of the most demented smiles Jake had ever seen. Not even Hollywood could make a beast look more horrible with all the make-up tricks in the world. Jake's blood ran cold, but he couldn't look away, like a car crash; the beast couldn't be ignored. Misery lifted the ear as if holding a trophy up for an audience before tossing it in his gaping maw like a peanut at the fair. He began to chew it while staring at Jake, daring him to look away. The bile that had built up at the back of Jake's throat came spewing out, shooting out of his mouth like a rocket coating him in his own sickness as he continued to gag after there was no fluid left to send flying.

Jake panted between gags, "FUCK. FUCK. FUCK YOU, SICK MOTHERFUCKER!" He croaked out the words more than yelling.

Jake's tirade stopped the beast's chewing for a moment as it frowned and bowed its head. This was only a temporary reprieve. Misery lifted his head laughing, forcing him to spew out gore and sending red stained spittle dribbling down his chin.

"Choke on it fuckstick!" Jake's courage momentarily resurfaced.

Misery didn't care for either the sentiment or the insult; Jake couldn't tell which, but the smile faded from his lips replaced with an animalistic sneer. The giant stepped forward, leaned down, grabbed Jake by the throat, and lifted him up until the leather straps holding him to the mattress creaked from the effort. The strangulation forced his eyes to bulge in the vice-like grip threatening to crush his trachea completely. Misery lifted Jake's entire body off the bed as though he were no more than a bug struggling to be free of a predator's grip. Jake was at the mercy of the merciless.

Misery continued to choke Jake with one had while cupping his left beneath his mouth. In an act of unspeakable abhorrence, he spat the remainder of the ear out into his palm. It was little more than a small pile of indistinguishable flesh, blood, and saliva now like a bit of raw hamburger. Jake knew what it was though, and the bile rose up his throat once more. Unable to vomit in Misery's chokehold, he began to choke. Misery lowered him back to the dirty mattress but relief was short-lived as the beast moved his right hand up squeezing his jaw forcing his mouth open. Quick as a flash, Misery slammed his left hand over Jake's gaping mouth forcing its grisly contents inside. Jake's eyes bulged in disgust as his jaw was slammed and held shut.

With his throat no longer constricted, the bitter bile bubbled up into his mouth mixing with the chewed up mass of his ear. Blood and bile dribbled from the corners of his mouth as he struggled with his abominable choice: choke and die, or swallow and breathe. It was no real choice, and Misery's eyes seemed to glow with satisfaction as the realization became visible on Jake's face. Jake swallowed with tears spilling from his eyes and bile burning his throat.

Misery's eyes practically glowed with the satisfaction at what he'd done while Dr. Pain cackled from behind the hulking mass like a witch at a comedy club. An evil sneer grew on the beast's lips as he watched Jake choke, gag, and cough on the impromptu meal. Next, without a word, Misery made a bad situation worse. He stepped back, unzipped his fly, and gave Jake something to wash down the ear stew.

Jake didn't even notice at first; his mind was consumed with the horror of what he had just been forced to do. All he wanted was to vomit up the meal, but it refused to oblige. He coughed and hacked, but nothing came out. His retching only made his already burning throat raw from the effort. This preoccupation ended as warm liquid entered his gaping mouth. He had forgotten his surroundings until he felt the stream hit his mouth. He instinctively swallowed before realizing the liquid's source. He slammed his mouth shut, but it was too late; his mouth was filled with the beast's urine.

'Repulsion' wasn't a strong enough word for how Jake felt, but he knew he was the embodiment of it. The beast's urine seemed to taste as bad as the thing's breath. Piss washed over his face for what seemed like forever but finally with a few last squirts Misery finished. Jake held his eyes shut tight, not daring to open them to let the urine sting and burn. He began to cough and gag desperately trying to vomit, but once again nothing happened. He had never been more disgusted, but still his stomach wouldn't release its vile contents.

"Tasty?" Dr. Pain asked. Jake had almost forgotten the good doctor in the madness.

"Go fuck yourself!" The words escaping Jake's mouth had lost any former defiance.

"Glad to see you can think of sex at a time like this. We may have to do something about that." Dr. Pain sounded as calm as ever, "What say you, Senor Misery, should we show the young man what happens to sex maniacs in OUR place?"

An insane smile was Misery's only answer. He then turned to the table lined with sadistic tools and rummaged around for a moment before turning around with a sharp, shiny long blade in his hands. Jake braced for the death blow, but it didn't come. Instead of stabbing him, Misery grabbed Jake's ankle ran the foot-long blade up the seam of the legs of his pants. Then, easy as pie, he threw the top layer to the side before ripping the bottom layer out from under his victim before tossing them to the back of the basement. Jake was left to lay on the filthy mattress in his silk boxer shorts stained from his own piss and blood from the slices made to his chest and belly.

What the fuck! Jake felt himself hyperventilating. *Calm down. Just breathe. Just breathe.* Then he heard Liam Neeson's voice pop in his head, *You're going to be raped. You can't fight it. This is what I want you to do: Cross your ankles and force your legs together. But I can't my ankles are strapped down!* Neeson's voice replied, *Then you're fucked.* Jake began to cry uncontrollably.

"Evangeline, where are you now?" Jake whispered, not realizing he had spoken out loud.

"Evangeline?" Dr. Pain queried.

"What?" Jake tried to play dumb now that he realized he had spoken aloud.

I won't let them get to you, angel. I may die down here, but I won't do that.

"So, that was her name. Ya know, she never did say. Kept crying out for you, though." Dr. Pain let the last word trail off for effect.

"LIAR! IF YOU HARM ONE HAIR ON HER HEAD, I WILL KILL YOU. I SWEAR I WILL KILL YOU!" Jake saw red at the thought of these animals torturing his beloved.

Dr. Pain crawled on top of Jake as slow as a lover until Jake's skin crawl. He slid up to Jake's chest crossing his hands to rest his head on. He stared directly into Jake's face, mocking affection as Jake struggled trying to throw the doctor off by twisting side to side. Dr. Pain just stared and smiled unmoved by the rocking.

"WHAT DID YOU DO MOTHERFUCKER!? GET THE FUCK OFF ME, YOU SONUVABITCH! I SWEAR IF YOU HURT HER, I WILL KILL YOU!" Jake knew his threats were empty, but they were all he had.

"She screamed so exquisitely. It was absolutely delightful." The doctor was grinning as he calmly whispered

"You haven't done shit! She's at home worrying about me is all." Jake didn't know if he was trying to convince himself or the doctor.

"I'm afraid not, sweetie. She is here. She's been waiting for you."

"Liar!" Jake shouted shakily.

"Oh, she was a delightful girl. At least that's what Misery tells me. He said he's never tasted anything sweeter." The doctor amused himself.

"You lie! You haven't done shit to her! She's far away from here. She's home waiting for me!"

"Do I detect a question?" The doctor was delighted in his own game. "It would seem you need some sort of proof. Your lover is here alright. She's right here with you in my hell. Though I'm afraid she's a tad worse for the wear. You understand."

"Evangeline!" Jake cried out knowing it was probably pointless, but if Evangeline was down here in this hell he wanted to see her.

"Unfortunately I don't think yelling is going to help you. I'm afraid she's…. um…. gone silent." With that, the good doctor rolled Jake to the back of the small room.

Jake's head was abuzz with everything from pain to disgust and was weighted down with the possibility that his love was down here suffering right along with him. The thought seemed impossible. He had put Evangeline on a plane not 2 days ago, or so he thought. How could she be down here in this hell being tortured by these sick bastards too? He began to hope for the best, but he then feared the worst. Doom hung over him like a storm cloud ready to break out in a torrential downpour with a fantastic light show.

Jake couldn't see any doors at the back of the room, but he could now hear ancient hinges crying out from lack of use. Dr. Pain pulled the door slowly and precisely for the nails-on-chalkboard effect. The chill it sent up Jake's spine lit each puncture on fire, but the pain from his missing ear far outweighed everything else. He couldn't see the doctor's smile, but he felt its weight on him . Then the doctor was out of sight.

After a moment of tormented silence, Jake began to hear a squeak emanate from the hidden room at the back of his prison cell like a shopping cart with a bad wheel. The squeak got louder until Jake could see a white sheet covering some sort of gurney poke through the doorway. As the good doctor pushed the squeaky gurney slowly forward, Jake began to see that the white sheet was spotted in dark red in several spots. There was no movement from underneath at all, not even the chest. Jake's heart sank the closer the gurney came. Whatever was under the sheet didn't seem to be alive. His sense of doom crept over him with every inch the gurney rolled on its noisy wheel.

The journey seemed to take hours but finally ended with the doctor pulling it even with the filthy mattress. Jake could see the sheet was stained with blood, but there were several other stains of indeterminable origin. Still, no movement came from beneath it. Whatever was being covered appeared to be dead or an inanimate object.

Oh my god. If she's under there she's dead. End of story. Please God, if you actually exist, please let it be someone else under that sheet. I beg you. Fuck, don't let it be my sweet Evangeline. If ever there was a God just don't let it be her!

Jake had barely finished begging God when Dr. Pain stepped to the front of the gurney and ripped the sheet off in one fell swoop like some demented magician. The horror that stared back at Jake was grotesque beyond his comprehension. He tried to scream, but it stuck in his throat. He stared wide-eyed with terror unable to scream, breathe or look away. The sight before him mesmerized and paralyzed him. He wanted desperately to look away but also wanted desperately to know if this was his sweet love or someone else.

"Go ahead sweetie, say a few words for your audience." Dr. Pain sneered out while ever so gently stroking the thing's raven black hair.

The thing's only reply was a bloody spit bubble or two blown from where its lips used to be. Jake's scream finally escaped his throat, long and powerful. Misery actually covered his ears while his pal Dr. Pain basked in its bloody glory as though standing before a symphony.

"Anguish never sounded so sweet!" The doctor cried out.

Chapter 4

The wind blew her hair across her face, giving her eyes the seductive look that drove him crazy. She was so beautiful. She was his angel: his babe, just his, and no one else's. Her emerald eyes gave her an exoticism that other women go to a doctor to achieve. Her raven black hair added a seductive mystery that men would kill to discover. Evangeline was the sort of beauty only imagined in fairy tales and, generally, only found there as well. Her father had called her God's masterpiece while Jake had settled on a much simpler term – angel.

Evangeline had come into Jake's life by what he thought was the greatest coincidence in the history of coincidences. He remembered every second of the chance encounter that had brought her into his life. It seemed fate had brought them together. Love finds a way was what Jake's father had always told him in regards to female relations. Jake never believed it until the day he met Evangeline.

Jake was on his way to work that cold November

morning, cursing the cold and life for making him suffer it. He walked up the steps of the subway to an arctic blast in his face with snow falling at what seemed a blizzard's pace. He hated the winter, longing for warmer climates, but Wall Street was in New York not Arizona. He could long for warmth all he wanted, he wasn't going to get it in November in New York City.

Jake grabbed the collar of his overcoat, shutting the cold and wind off from his exposed throat as much as possible. With a Gucci briefcase in his right hand, he leaned into the wind trying to keep his balance as he began the short trek from the subway outlet to the warmth of his office only a block away. The cold wind forced him to squint until his eyelids were barely open. Jesus, he fucking hated the cold and the snow, especially when they're together! The grimace on his face could be mistaken for pain in another surrounding, but here the same look was plastered across everyone's face.

He had wanted to run to the warmth of his building, but New York City at 7:30am made running no more than wishful thinking. The crowd was shoulder to shoulder which fortunately blocked some of the cold wind, but not much to his lament. After an agonizing few minutes, Jake finally reached the lobby doors of Dimon Bank & Trust. He pushed through the revolving doors yearning for the warmth on the other side. He took a few steps inside so as to get out of the way of everyone else coming through, then he stood there for a moment soaking up the heat he had so longed for on his short journey.

He just stood there for a moment, eyes closed, trying to bring himself back to life with the warmth. The ache slowly melted from his joints as he stood there oblivious to the world around him. A serenity washed over him, as he stood there content to bask in its glow.

As he stood there obliviously enjoying his moment,

he was nearly knocked off his feet from behind. His eyes popped wide as he spun around ready to give a piece of his mind to the fool who had dared to spoil his moment.

"Hey, what the f…?" His words trailed off as he stood face to face with his "attacker."

"Oh my God, I'm so sorry. Are you okay? I didn't hurt you did I?" The voice was as beautiful as the lips emitting them.

Jake stood there slack jawed on the verge of drooling. The beauty that had nearly toppled him over was saying something, but he didn't care what the words were. He didn't even know who this beauty was, yet but already he was putty in her hands.

"I said are you okay?" She asked while shaking his shoulder slightly. "What's your name?" Jake heard the words but all he could do was stare.

He was snapped back to the real world when she smacked him lightly but sternly across the cheek.

"Hey what's the idea?" He said with no real anger rubbing his cheek.

"Well you seemed catatonic. I had to do something. Now, are you alright?" Her voice nearly put him in a trance once more.

"Wha… uh, well… er, I'm sorry, what were you saying?" Jake's disorientation made him seem concussed.

"Are you okay?" The woman over-enunciated every syllable carefully as if speaking to a foreigner or a mentally challenged person.

"Yes, yes. I'm sorry. Guess I'm just a little off this morning. Are you alright?" Jake's senses finally returned, though he was mesmerized by the woman.

"I'm fine. I'm the one who plowed into you, if you remember." Her voice sang.

"Well, being bumped by you seems to be more of an

honor than an assault. I'm Jacob, by the way."

"Evangeline. Evangeline Shamaya." She reached a hand out to him as she gave him her full name.

"Pleasure to meet you, Evangeline Shamaya." He grabbed her hand lightly afraid she would shatter like glass if he gripped too hard.

"Well, not that pleasurable given that I nearly knocked you over. I'd say the pleasure is all mine." She flashed her perfect eyelashes at him as he let go of her hand.

"I don't think I've seen you here before, is there anything I can help you with? I am a senior VP here after all, and it seems you have me at your disposal at the moment." He prayed that she needed his assistance. He was not ready for this chance meeting to end just yet.

"So you're the boss, huh?"

"In a manner of speaking, I guess you could say I'm the boss." He flashed Evangeline his best smile.

"Well then, I was actually hoping to talk to someone about my small investment portfolio. I have an appointment with a Mr. Karrigan, I think it is."

"Karrigan's a good man, one of my best actually. Can I show you to his office?" He prayed she needed him just a bit longer.

"That would be wonderful actually. I've never been to his office before and it's a bit, uh, more than I expected. This place is amazing."

Until Evangeline had mentioned it, Jake had forgotten how daunting even just the lobby of Dimon Bank & Trust could be. The lobby was gigantic. There was a two-story waterfall at the center of the lobby, which was beautiful though somewhat gaudy. Expensive artwork hung on every wall and there was nowhere one could turn without seeing DIMON BANK & TRUST in huge faux diamond lettering. They were gaudy, nearly vomit inducing to anyone with taste. For James Dimon, it was no secret that he had no taste whatsoever.

"Yeah I forget how, um, breathtaking it can be if you've never seen it before." Jake held back further comment on how hideousness he found it all.

"Does it make you want to vomit as much as I do right now?" Evangeline gave voice to the thought in his head.

"Well, um, well I… uh… Now that you mention it that is exactly what I think about it. A little, erm… gaudy I guess." He kept his voice low looking around to make sure no one was within earshot as he made his confession.

"I think we're going to get along just fine Jacob, just fine indeed."

***

The memory imprints were his shrine creating a fog that blurred out his pain and reality. Their first meeting, their first kiss, their first time in bed, and everything in between created a circle of serenity that was impenetrable to the world outside Jacob Falgoust's mind. Given his situation, it was more of a memory mausoleum sealing him away from pain and all that was still to come. His euphoric moment wouldn't last, but a slight reprieve was better than none to his mind.

"So what do you think of my masterpiece, dearest boy? Better, no?" Dr. Pain's voice hit Jake like a slap to the face.

Jake felt the tears streaming down his cheeks. Any remnants of his tough guy defiance from earlier was all but gone. His resistance was gone. There was only room here for despair, hopelessness, and of course, horrendous pain.

His back ached from the weeping polka dot punctures, his left hand throbbed from his missing finger, his head pounded with every pulse from his missing ear, and any hope of escape or rescue had left him like rats from a burning building. He was an abject failure, not being able to keep himself nor his beautiful Evangeline safe from this horror filled basement. He closed his eyes unable to look at the grotesquery his angel beside him had become.

"Cat got yer tongue, boy? What do you think of my work of art? Some artists work in paint or clay, but meat makes a much better canvas. Wouldn't you agree?" Dr. Pain could barely constrain his laughter at his own sick humor.

Ignoring something doesn't make it go away, but it was all Jake could do. He desperately tried to retrieve an image of his lovely Evangeline from his memory library to block out his reality. He knew it was in his mind somewhere, but all he could see was the bloody thing lying beside him. A bright red, dripping sack of meat was the only image filling his brain now. His torturer had won. Seeing his love any other way was as impossible of stopping an asteroid collision; it was going to happen and there wasn't a Goddamn thing he could do about it. He forced his eyes open confined to seeing his emerald eyed angel for what the demented doctor had made of her.

The bloody mass on the gurney next to him was barely recognizable as human. Evangeline's raven black hair and curves were all that distinguished her body from a pile of hamburger beef. Those otherworldly green eyes were all that remained of his angel. Dr. Pain had meticulously removed her skin, skin Jake remembered being as soft as down feathers. The love of his life had been reduced to a bloody, anatomically correct doll for teaching unrecognizable as the true beauty she had been.

"Evangeline?" Jake whispered hoping that death had come to put her out of her misery.

Another bloody bubble escaped her lips but no more.

Tears flowed harder while he blew his own bubbles from his nose as sorrow overtook him. 'Atrocious' was the word that came to his mind as he looked at the epitome of atrocious. A wave of repulsion washed over him while gazing at the remains of his love threatening to send his stomach contents spewing forth. Thoughts of his own torturous future filled his head and for a brief moment the grotesquery before him faded away. In that moment, doubt disguised as hope crept into his mind. Perhaps this thing wasn't really his Evangeline; maybe, just maybe, it was someone else. It couldn't be Evangeline. *I put her on a plane at JFK just two days ago,* he thought. There was no way this was his love.

Think damn it. Maybe they picked up someone else with black hair and beautiful green eyes. Maybe this is just a hoax to scare you. It has to be! It just has to be!

"Evangeline!" Jake shouted her name at the top of his lungs.

"Evangeline! Evangeline! Evangeline! That's right, scream her name! Scream it!" The doctor's mockery shook Jake back to reality.

"It's not her. It's not her you sick fuck. You're trying to fuck with my head but guess what, FUCK YOU!" Jake spat the words at his tormenter.

"Now, now boy. Just look at her. Your eyes aren't deceiving you, Jacob. Would you like to know if she begged for you? Would you like to know how loud she screamed? Or perhaps you would like to know how she tastes? I assure you, she's quite delicious." Dr. Pain let the last words roll slowly off his tongue.

"Fuck you! You… you sick, twisted Fuck! Just shut your fucking mouth. It's not her. It can't be her she left town on a fucking plane I put her on asshole so take your bullshit and go fuck Igor over there!" Jake's defiance was making a resounding comeback.

"You're a really smart, huh? Let me ask you this

smart guy, how long have you been here in my home? One, two, maybe three days? Or has it been longer? You need to ask yourself these things, Jacob. I mean, just how long does it take an artist to create such a wondrous work? Perhaps the more pertinent question that you should have in mind, Jacob, is what does that artist have in store for me?"

"Fuc—" Jake's defiance was immediately cut off by Misery slamming the ball gag into his mouth once again.

"Misery, be careful with our guest. We don't want to hurt him… yet." The giant yellow-toothed grin returned to light up the doctor's face.

Misery's blow knocked Jake unconscious. The blow wouldn't keep him out long, though. Misery repositioned him for his master. He enjoyed the game like a fat kid enjoys chocolate cake. Dr. Pain was king in their basement kingdom, and it was time to get to work.

Chapter 5

The elevator doors closed on their sole occupants, leaving them in the awkward silence of strangers. The two occupants stood silent, both wanting to break it. Her beauty made him forget all about how much he had been cursing the day not five minutes earlier. She lifted him to a different world full of bright sunshine and daisies without any cares or worries.

Finally, she broke the silence. "So how long have you been a banker?"

"A banker? Well let me see, I started in the mailroom when I was 18 so that would make it… well… let's just say, longer than I care to admit." He let out a sigh with a smile that couldn't have been removed with sandpaper.

"So just a couple of years then?" Evangeline flirted.

"Let's just say more than a couple but less than a lifetime."

"That's quite a range. Are you trying to make me guess?"

"No, no. There's no shame in my game. I've worked

my way up over the last 15-ish years to reach the cushy office job I've always wanted. So, what about you? What is it someone as lovely as you does for a living? Model perhaps?"

"A little of this, little of that. I used to model, but I had to get out of that scene. Nothing but pretentiousness and drugs at the pro-level, so I quit and now I'm here with a handsome gentleman leading me to what I hope will be someone that will help me instead of steal my life savings." She finished with a sultry wink as the elevator stopped.

"It's just down the hall there, Suite 5224." Jake stated as Evangeline stepped off the elevator.

"And where is your office, Jacob?" She prodded.

"Mine? Next floor, Suite 5316. Come see me when you're done. Maybe we could grab a cup of coffee or something before you head back home." Jake sent up the most desperate prayer of his life hoping that she would say yes.

"Only if you agree to spend our time apart thinking about me and only me, can you do that?" Jake had never heard anything more seductive in his life.

"I shall try my best." Jake had to swallow back a lump that had suddenly materialized in his throat.

"You had better do more than try. Maybe this will help." She grabbed his wrist and rubbed it with her own. "There, now if you stop thinking of me you can just sniff your way back on track."

His heart literally skipped a beat. He already couldn't bear the wait. Evangeline was a vision out of a dream, one he couldn't bear to wake from, "Um, while I appreciate the gesture, why don't we go now? That way I can't possibly forget about you." He was too anxious, but he had to try.

"But how will you know if you miss me if we never part?" Evangeline's flirting skills were far superior to any woman Jake had ever met.

"Honestly, I miss you already."

"Parting is such sweet sorrow. Goodbye Jacob." She had the most seductive, mischievous smile Jake had ever seen. She turned and started down the hall shaking her perfect behind knowing full well what it would do to him.

"Suite 5316. Don't forget, I'll be waiting!" Jake called out, though she didn't acknowledge him.

He stepped back into the elevator letting the doors close feeling dejected. A one floor trip had never seemed so long. He stepped off at his floor and made the journey to his office with his head hung low wondering if he would see Evangeline Shamaya again.

Jake passed his secretary without looking up as she wished him good morning, going straight to his chair while unable to get Evangeline out of his mind. He lifted his wrist up to his nose, inhaling deeply which made him smile like a half-wit. *So, angels smell of rose water,* he thought.

The minutes passed like days as he waited patiently for her to return to him. Fear set in as the morning faded toward noon with no sign of her. He answered a few phone calls, but was able to do little else as he waited impatiently. He inhaled the scent on his wrist repeatedly, breathing it in like it was the essence of life itself. The wait was beginning to drive him insane, though he suspected that was part of her game.

Then she was suddenly back. Jake had to pinch himself to make sure he wasn't dreaming. There was something about this woman that made him feel as if his dull life suddenly had meaning. The urge to run to her took hold, but he knew it would be inappropriate and he would probably scare her off. The wait was killing him; he was sure she knew as well.

"It's okay Mrs. Summers, you can let her in." His

voice was noticeably shaky even through the intercom.

An eternity passed before the door to his office finally opened, revealing Evangeline in all her beauty. He knew in that moment there was nothing he wouldn't do for her. He would crawl across a mile of broken glass to be with her if she asked. Most people lived their entire lives never finding true love. Jacob Falgoust knew now he could no longer be counted among their numbers.

***

"Wakey, wakey. You may want to stay very still." The doctor's screechy voice and gutter breath wiped out the memory Jake had been enjoying faster than a lightning strike.

Pain was the first thing to hit Jake returning him to reality. The ball gag Misery had strapped in his mouth had mercifully been removed. The vision of his precious angel was extinguished completely. His wounds were on fire as he dared to look at his mangled angel. Anger as he had never felt washed over him like a flood turning to an unquenchable rage. He had never harmed a fly, but now he longed for an opportunity to put the instruments laid out on the table to work on these two demons.

"EVANGELINE!" He yelled out in anger and frustration.

"I don't think she can hear you, my dear boy. I fear she has finally moved on." Dr. Pain took immense pleasure informing Jake of his lover's demise. "It appears she has crossed over to the other side, if you believe in such nonsense."

"I'll kill you! I swear I will kill you, you son of a bitch! Evangeline!" Jake yelled out.

The doctor smiled so broad that Jake could see every one of the good doctor's disgusting yellow teeth. The doctor advanced slowly on his victim, running his finger gently down Evangeline's body like caressing a lover. Jake cringed, appalled by Evangeline's body being desecrated. He watched in horror as the doctor's finger slid from his love's heel, up her calf, to her thigh pausing with a little swirl on her hip before sliding between her legs. The doctor lingered, making sure Jake knew exactly what he was doing. Finally, the doctor continued to caress her abdomen up to her sagging breasts where he paused once more for effect. He ended by lifting up Evangeline's head to stroke her silky black hair, never once unlocking his eyes from Jacob's. Jake strained against his bonds with all his might. He wanted to tear the doctor limb-by-limb with his bare hands. He wanted to shower in the man's blood as his own boiled in his veins.

"Take a good long look." The doctor whispered inches from Jake's face again, "Her suffering was glorious, yours will be divine!"

"Fuck You!" Jake whispered with a growl as he tried to inhale as little of his tormentor's foul breath as possible.

"Oh, poor boy, I'm afraid all the fucking in this room was all used up on your little girlfriend." The doctor turned back to stroke Evangeline's hair once more, "I'm afraid my, um, large assistant just about wore the poor little thing out. She begged and pleaded for you to come save her, but you didn't, did you? My eager assistant did, many times, but you… you never came." Dr. Pain sounded exactly like Emperor Palatine from Star Wars.

"I swear, I will find a way to kill you for this."

"So you're ready to begin then?" Dr. Pain sneered, "Misery, please take my bloody Juliet back to its place so we may begin on Romeo."

Without a word, Misery rose from where he was

crouching at the back of the basement to do as asked. He grabbed the end of the gurney with one large meat hook but before wheeling it out. He took a moment to gloat. He looked down at Jake and shot him a dastardly grin as he adjusted his manhood with his free hand. He savored his little torment like a fine wine before pulling Juliet to the back room.

As soon as his henchman had wheeled out the artwork, the doctor pulled a wooden chair between his victim and his table of tools. There were no restraints that Jake could make out on the chair, though he had no doubt that he was to be fastened to the old wooden chair in some fashion momentarily. It appeared to be ancient with its once dark stain worn nearly bare in several spots. Jake tried not to think about how the finish had been worn off, though it was impossible for him not to think about what coming next.

After a few minutes the hulking Misery returned heading straight to Jake on the filthy mattress. Fire spit from Jake's eyes as the beast grabbed him by the hand with the missing finger. The thing's vice-like grip set his stump alight with pain. Misery unfastened the leather wrist bindings, bringing Jake's hands tight together with one of his oversized hands as he unfastened the restraints around his ankles. Once finished, Misery grabbed Jake by the throat while still holding his hands fast. In one motion, he lifted Jake off the bed, turned, and flung him into the chair with force.

Jake felt as if he had been hit in the gut by a wrecking ball. He doubled over in the chair trying to find his breath. Still reeling, Misery grabbed a wrist in each hand and slammed them onto the arms of the chair with bone crushing force. He then stomped first his left foot, then his right, onto Jake's feet to hold him in place with their faces only an inch apart.

Once he caught his breath, Jake realized the doctor's

breath was like a refreshing spring breeze in comparison. Misery smelled as if he had eaten and then rolled in some rotting road kill covered in feces with hot garbage gravy.. Bile rose into his throat again, burning a path to his mouth. The desire for death overflowed from within. Misery was blocking him from seeing what the doctor was up to, though he didn't want to know anyway.

A nail drove through his hand into the arm of the chair with one swift blow. The shock forced the bile rising in his throat all over Misery's face. Before he caught his breath from the first blow, a second spike drove through his other hand. Jake would have bit his own tongue off if Misery hadn't punched him in the throat Jake gasped for air like an asthmatic fish out of water. When you can't breathe every second, it feels like a hundred as the mind loses all rational thought in its panic for oxygen. Jake convulsed straining every muscle in his body until his diaphragm finally relented, allowing him to fill his lungs with precious air.
Oxygen rushed in along with intense agony. Before Jake could begin to enjoy his relief, Misery grabbed his ankle as the doctor, with one powerful swing, pounded a rusty spike through the top of his foot and secured it to the chair. The white hot pain had him gasping for air once again as the treatment was repeated on his left foot. The spikes through his hands had hurt, but the ones through his feet were like red hot lava still burning his flesh. He vomited, missing Misery this time, and wet himself for the second time. He was now one with the chair. They were inseparable. *I'm finally dead*, Jake thought before returning into the darkness once again.

Chapter 6

"Sorry I took so long. Would you like to grab some lunch rather than just a coffee?" Evangeline's voice was like an angel singing to Jake's ears.

"Well, um, sure. Did you have something in mind, or are we winging it?"

"Since I don't know this area very well, I guess we're winging it. Unless you have something in mind, that is?" She gave him a slight wink causing Jake's heart to skip a beat.

"Actually, I do." He gave her a wink of his own as he grabbed his coat from the rack by his desk.

The fledgling lovers made their way back to the gaudy lobby and out the front door. Jake hailed a cab instructing the driver where to go as he climbed in alongside his new-found beauty.

"Would you do me a quick favor?" He asked her coyly.

"Depends on the favor." She answered with a smile.

"I was hoping you would pinch me so that I know

I'm not dreaming right now."

She gave him a little pinch on the back of his arm as she put her lips a hair's breadth from his ear. "You're definitely not dreaming."

Jake's heart fluttered like a schoolboy as his cheeks flushed. He hadn't realized he was smiling like an idiot, though he was helpless to do anything about it. He had never felt luckier in all his days. Despite Evangeline's reassurance, he thought he must be dreaming (if only his dreams had ever been this good).

Then Evangeline sealed the deal, "What say we skip lunch."

Without hesitation Jake called out, "Driver, please take us to The Plaza instead. Thank You."

***

A hard slap brought Jake back to his grim reality and stole his love from him once again. Evangeline's beautiful visage was replaced with the wretched vileness of his tormenting scum. Consciousness brought his pain back in full force. Every cell in his body was screaming, but there was something else: a new pain below his chin. Fear caused him to hyperventilate increasing his agony further.

"Calm yourself Jacob. You're gonna need your energy." The doctor whispered in his ear again.

"Wha…" Jake tried to speak, but something sharp stabbed him under his chin.

"Careful now." The doctor whispered, "Feel that little poke? Choose your words carefully. This little thing makes every word precious." The doctor flicked something metallic under Jake's chin.

"Let me go asshole!" Jake clenched his teeth trying not to stab himself again.

"Now, you've got the idea! Careful, be very careful,

Jacob. Would you like to see what you're wearing?" Dr. Pain let out a demented chuckle with the question.

Dr. Pain didn't wait for any reply. He adjusted the mobile surgical light to fully illuminate Jake's head. The mirror he held up was grimy, but Jake could see what was stabbing him: a leather strap wrapped around his neck with a twin-tined, double-sided fork fastened to it. The upper two tines pressed into the underside of his chin while the tines on the opposite end rested at the crux between his neck and collarbone. In the time of the Inquisition, the device had been dubbed the heretic's fork. It was a favorite device of inquisitors since it could cause massive pain but rarely fatal injuries.

"What the fuck is this? Get this thing the fuck off me!" Jake spit out through his clenched jaw.

"I'm sorry, that's not an option right now. Please take some solace in the fact that you're getting off easy. In this tool's heyday the wearer generally had their hands bound behind them. Then they would be hung by those hands from a hook in the ceiling. The discomfort was, shall we say… intense." The doctor moved in close to whisper, "Count the little blessings Jacob Falgoust."

The doctor's idea of a blessing seemed to differ greatly from that of his victim. Jake knew there were no blessings to be counted down here in this hell: Evangeline was dead, and he longed to join her. He prayed to a god he didn't even believe in for the end to come quickly. The only reprieve he found was in trying to arch his head back to relieve the fork stabbing into him in four different places. It was precious little relief, but it was all he was going to get.

While Jake prayed for death, the doctor set the mirror aside before grabbing another odd device off the table. The device hadn't been designed with torture in mind, but the doctor found it worked quite well in that capacity. In its medical life it had been known as an artificial leech invented in the mid-1840s for bloodletting, which doctors and barbers for centuries believed cured a wide variety of ailments. The device was six-inches long with sharp steel points protruding from one end leading into a cylinder with a pump at the opposite end to suck out blood from the circular hole made by pressing the points into the skin and twisting in a circle. The user, in this case Dr. Pain, could suck out as much blood as he wished from the patient. Though it was never intended for torture, the doctor found it was very useful in such a regard to slowly bleed a patient in a controlled manner. Without warning, the doctor slammed the artificial leech into his Jake's chest slightly below the left nipple. He held it there a moment before twisting it slowly in a full circle. He enjoyed the torment. Jake screamed, forcing the tines deep into his flesh.

"Poor form, Jacob. Now that really had to hurt. Do try to keep your fucking mouth shut for a minute while I work." The doctor said never raising his voice a single octave.

"Please, just stop. Please." The plea was as weak as its speaker.

"Sorry Jacob, but this won't be over quickly and you won't enjoy this." Again, the doctor took great pleasure in the words he spoke so calmly.

"Please." Jake's plea was worthless.

Dr. Pain ignored him to continue his game. "Now, what we have here is a very old doctor's tool, though not nearly as ancient as that heretic's fork on your neck. This one wasn't invented until about 1840. Can you guess its name, Jacob?" The doctor delighted in his torments.

"Go fuck yourself." Jake spat out.

The tears streaming from his eyes stung as they mixed with the fresh wounds under his chin while increasing the pain in the wound that was once his ear. He attempted to conjure Evangeline in his mind but the pain would spare no room for her.

"Tsk, tsk. Jacob, my dear boy, you really need to learn the virtue of silence. Perhaps I can help you with that." Dr. Pain slowly pulled the plunger of the leeching device to emphasize his point.

A few ounces of blood rolled down Jake's chest, pooling between his legs. Dr. Pain pulled the artificial leech from Jake's chest with an audible pop then motioned Misery to come forward. Jake braced for the worst. Misery approached from behind the chair, receiving a disapproving glance from the doctor for reasons Jake didn't understand — but Misery did. He moved around kneeling in front of Jake, leaning forward until his chin rested on Jake's forehead. The doctor stood over them, emptying what blood remained in the artificial leech into the open mouth of Misery, bringing bile racing back into Jake's throat.

Crimson gushed down over Misery's face into his gaping maw. Jake tried to pull back, but he only drove the fork deeper. As the doctor forced the plunger down, Jake's blood overflowed Misery's mouth and trickled down his massive chin all over Jake. The rain of his own blood mixed with his sweat, tears, and old blood as it rolled over him.

With the chamber empty, Misery moved as the doctor slammed the infernal contraption into Jake's chest to repeat the procedure. Dr. Pain continued until Jake began to fade away from blood loss. The doctor knew when to stop, leaving Jake alone in his hell terrorizing himself with thoughts of what was to come next. Jake's conscious faded with no will left. He longed for his Evangeline to be away from this place.

Chapter 7

The sweet smell of passion hung in the air of the The Plaza Suite like dense fog. *This had, without a doubt, been the best day of my life,* Jake thought. He had forgotten cursing the day as he stepped out of the subway that morning. Now, here he was with the most beautiful woman he could have imagined. Sometimes, the day just never goes the way you expect.

He could hear her singing in the shower and was tempted to join her, but she had forbade it. So, instead, he just had to imagine the water glistening over her perfect breasts and that wonderfully perfect ass. He could see her in his mind's eye as clear as day, and the vision was stunning. He felt himself getting aroused, but he didn't care. He hoped the afternoon wasn't over yet.

Evangeline emerged from the bathroom fully dressed and ready to leave. Disappointed, Jake knew he had to get back to work as well before someone realized just how long he had been gone. He thought he'd try to convince her to stay a bit longer though.

"The bed's getting cold my dear." He said patting the mattress beside him.

Evangeline just stared at him a moment until he thought she was just going to walk out and he'd never see her again. His heart climbed into his throat until finally she replied, "I have places to be and so do you." Her tone was so matter of fact he feared this was a one-time thing.

"Wi…will I see you again?" He croaked like a teenage boy.

She stared a moment then asked, "Well that depends, do you have dinner plans?"

"Nothing." He said relieved.

"Good! Then I'll meet you at Alfredo's at 7, but you have to promise me something." As she spoke she walked to the edge of the bed.

"Anything."

Evangeline bent over him until her lips were only millimeters from his. Then looking him straight in the eyes whispered, "You must think of me every second from now til then."

"Deal. But will you think of me?"

Evangeline kissed him lightly replying seductively, "That's hard." She grabbed his manhood giving it a soft squeeze then left him hanging.

If asked this morning, Jake would have said he didn't believe in love at first site. Now, he was sold hook, line, and sinker. Waiting five hours to see her again was going to be torturous; the minutes were sure to crawl by. He sank back onto the bed in wonderment, wanting to savor their afternoon together before returning to the real world where work was waiting for him. Reluctantly, he headed back to his office, a pointless endeavor as he wasn't likely to get anything done but it did kill time.

Once back in his office, he instructed his secretary to

make the reservation at Alfredo's and entered his office to stare at the clock for the next few hours. The day dragged just as he suspected. A few mundane conference calls, several e-mails, and some pencil pushing. Then it was finally five o'clock and time to head out.

Jake called his car service to pick him up rather than waste time on the subway. He had decided to get a new suit for his dinner date then perhaps pick out something special for Evangeline too. *Earrings or maybe a necklace*, he thought, *would be a nice gesture. Not too much and not too little*. He'd give her the world if that's what she wanted. He was head over heels for the first time in his life.

He walked in the restaurant a full half-hour early, only to find Evangeline already waiting for him. It took every ounce of his will not to sprint to her. He felt as giddy as a school girl. He managed to maintain his composure and calmly walked to the bar to join his beauty waiting for their table. She was even more stunning than he had remembered. All he wanted was to finish the formality of dinner so they could get back to the suite and never leave.

***

Whack!

An open palmed smack from Misery and his angel was gone. Jake felt woozy as though he were still asleep or drunk. He didn't know how much blood the doctor had drained from him, but unfortunately it hadn't been enough to allow him to fade out of existence quite yet. It felt like the worst hangover of his life.

"Welcome back Jacob." The doctor's sinister grin greeted him, "We missed you."

A weak grunt was all Jake was able to manage in

response. There were at least a dozen circular wounds weeping streaks of red across his chest and abdomen. He instinctively attempted to wipe the blood away forgetting he was nailed to the old wooden chair. He was on the verge of passing out again which was his only escape from this hell. He could hear Evangeline calling to him.

"Here, drink this." The doctor held out a paper cup filled with orange juice, unwittingly flinging Evangeline back into darkness.

Before Jake could reply, Misery grabbed him by the hair and pulled his head back to relieve the pressure of the heretic's fork though it was little consolation. Misery gripped his jaw, forcing his mouth open as the doctor poured the juice into his mouth. Fearing it may be poison, or worse, Jake tried to spit the liquid out. Misery ended the effort by slamming his jaw shut with teeth, shattering force and holding his nose giving him no choice but to swallow.

"No need to fear, Jacob. It's only orange juice. Save your strength, you're going to need it." The doctor spoke calmly as Jake gulped down the juice. "Good! Suck it all down. That's good."

The cup empty, the doctor crushed and tossed it to the back of the basement. Dr. Pain pulled up a chair in front of Jake, leaving only a few inches between their knees. Jake found having the doctor so close disconcerting at best.

"Did you get enough juice?" The doctor asked in a friendly tone.

"Eat shit!"

Dr. Pain ignored the insult, "Now, we're gonna play a little game. Do you like games, Jacob?"

Jake refused to answer hoping the doctor would just kill him ending this nightmare. He tried imagining that this was all just a nightmare, that he'd soon wake from with his angel beside him. He knew it was false hope, but that's all he had left otherwise there was only pain.

"How about a riddle Jacob? Do you like riddles? If you can answer one little riddle, I'll let you go, if not… well, your journey to this point will seem like tiptoeing through the tulips as the man once said. You have my word, Jacob. Answer my riddle and you'll go free." The doctor had never sounded more devious.

"And if I refuse? What then?"

"Oh, you're going to play Jacob. However, your level of participation is entirely up to you." The doctor accentuated his point with his sinister yellow toothed grin.

Dr. Pain reached into the pocket of his lab coat and produced a pair of small pruning shears used for clipping small branches and such. They were rusty though the edge and they shined in the light . The doctor held the shears up, opening and closing the blades to taunt his victim.

"Now, thanks to my large friend, you've only got nineteen chances instead of twenty to answer correctly. I should warn you, failure to answer counts as an incorrect response. I'll give you a hint though, the answer has already been provided to you, so I hope you've been paying attention! Are you ready to get started?" The doctor sounded like the most demented game show host in history.

"I'm not playing your fucking game, asshole!" Jake yelled as loud as he could without stabbing himself on the fork.

"Jacob, I think you weren't paying attention. We're playing, end of story. Now, the game is quite simple, Jacob. All you have to do is answer my question. Answer correctly, Misery and I will happily escort you straight out the front door to your freedom. Answer incorrectly, you lose one digit. Seeing as how you only have nineteen digits, you only have nineteen chances. There is no phone a friend option, so you're all on your own. Ready, Jacob?" Dr. Pain ended with a cackle which Misery mimicked from behind Jake.

"I don't want to play." Jake was reduced to whining.

"Nobody ever wants to play Jacob, but it'll be fun! Just think you have the opportunity to win your freedom. Sure, you'll be missing a little finger and a lover, but you can be free." Dr. Pain clearly enjoyed his taunts.

"Why? Why me? I've never harmed anyone or anything. I'm innocent." Though sincere, Jake felt as whiny as he sounded.

"That, my dear Jacob, will be answered shortly. Now, let's begin!"

Jake's only answer was silence, seeing no point in saying anything else. Misery had moved beside him, grabbed his hand, and pressed his fingers out flat. The force drove liquid fire shooting up Jake's arm; the stump of his pinky finger throbbed like a jackhammer.

"Hang on Misery, bring the iron first!" Dr. Pain scolded his assistant with disdain.

The momentary release only made the stump throb worse, which was a distraction from every other aching part of his body. Jake wished they would kill him and be done with it, but a quick death wasn't coming. He didn't want to think about what was in store for him by the time this was all over.

Misery returned all too soon with a red hot iron in his meaty grip. It was not a modern electric iron but an old one made of solid iron. Old ones like this had to be heated over a fire or set on a stove top. Jake could see the one in Misery's hand was white with heat. His eyes bulged out of their sockets as the doctor's spit sizzled on the flat surface like a meat on a frying pan. The spittle was reduced to a small white stain almost instantly.

Dr. Pain smiled at him, "We can't have you bleeding out before the game is through, Jacob. Nineteen chances, ready?"

"Fuck you!" The fork's tines jabbing him almost made him regret his defiance.

"Good! First and only question, what is lower than the devil? First chance." The doctor sounded like a demonic Bob Barker.

"What?" Jake asked.

"Wrong answer!" Dr. Pain delighted in snapping the pruning shears shut on Jake's ring finger.

The finger dropped to the floor with a plop as blood shot from the stump Misery wasted no time pressing the hot iron to the wound, enjoying the sound and smell of Jake's sizzling flesh. The sadistic pair found the whole situation hilarious.

Dr. Pain repositioned the shears around Jake's middle finger. He called out with joy, "Eighteen more chances! Misery, please put ten seconds on the clock. Jacob, what is lower than the devil?" Dr. Pain licked his lips in anticipation. "10,9,8…"

"You! You sick fuck!" Jake regretted the instigation instantly as he watched his middle finger fall to the floor, spurting crimson weakly. "Fuuuuuuuuuucccccccccckkkkkkkk!" The outburst forced all four fork tines deep into his tender flesh.

Before Jake's scream finished resonating off the walls, Misery grabbed the iron and cauterized the wound, ending any further protest. Dr. Pain lifted a vile of smelling salts to Jake's nose to keep him from passing out cold again.

Hold yourself together man. You can do this. Think. What is the answer to Insane-O's fucking question? What the fuck does this ass face think is lower than the devil? What!?!

The shears were readied at his forefinger. "Ten

seconds! Now, what is lower than the devil? And Go!" Dr. Pain continued his sick Bob Barker impression.

"Your assfaced buddy! Misery!"

The shears clamped shut dropping his forefinger to the floor. Blood spurted, and Misery laughed as he burned the wound closed.

"Last chance for this poor hand Jacob. What is lower than the devil? Tick Tock!"

"I don't fucking know!"

His thumb dropped to the floor followed by a quick cauterization as the game continued chewing up fingers. He could find no answer through the pain as his mind could think of nothing other than death. Dr. Pain and Misery weren't about to allow it, at least not yet. One-by-one, his snipped fingers caused horrendous pain, but he dreaded his toes even more knowing they were far more sensitive.

The doctor produced a syringe from his pocket and introduced it, "This is adrenaline Jacob." He flicked the syringe. "I can't have you passing out in the middle of such a fun game. Ten chances left, time to dig deep Jacob."

Jake had never tried cocaine, but he imagined this is what it must feel like. His heart pounded so hard in his chest he thought it may explode, making every one of his stubs throb horribly. All other pain was lost in the dissonant screams from the ten little stumps. Misery had exited to heat the iron, leaving Jake alone with his pain and the evil that had caused it. There was no joy in the small reprieve with the adrenaline coursing through Jake's veins. Tears streamed from his eyes uncontrollably as he prayed for a death that was continuing to elude him.

"While we have a minute, Jacob, perhaps you should use the time thinking of a better answer. You're running out of digits. I'm told toes are much more painful." The doctor shook his head. "You really should know the answer, Jacob. I'm quite disappointed."

"Fuck you, motherfucker! You're the only thing worse than the devil!" Jake didn't care if there would be a reprisal, yelling alleviated the pain for a fraction of a second.

"Worse? No, no Jacob. Lower, lower than the devil. Now think. You might also consider that there are worse things I can get off of you Jacob. You haven't even begun to shake hands with pain yet. Think about it, Jacob Falgoust." Dr. Pain seemed to lose his temper for a moment, "I've shown you the answer. Ten chances left." The doctor sneered at him as though disgusted by his presence.

Jake was stunned into silence. He had never felt so utterly hated. Before he could ponder further, the door opened; Misery re-entered Jacob Falgoust's hell. The iron was glowing bright red as the monster set it on its tray beside the doctor. Jake wept, not ready to begin again.

"Now for the tenth time, the million dollar question, ten seconds on the clock, Jacob, what is lower than the devil?" Dr. Pain restarted the game with his shears encompassing Jake's left pinky toe.

"I don't fucking know! Please, just let me go!"

"Wrong again!" A snip and the small toe fell to the floor as Misery leaned in to burn the wound closed, "Again. What is your answer?"

Jake answered with silence followed by a snip and a burn before the cycle repeated. Jake had no answer. *What could possibly be lower than the devil?* He thought. He was being tortured by the only two possible answers to his mind. Eight tries left, but it didn't matter if he had a million.

Snip. Burn. Question. Silence. Snip. Burn. Question. The cycle kept repeating until Dr. Pain had snipped his way to the big toe. Jake resorted to praying for the answer but found none. He was drunk with pain, making it near impossible to think. He racked his brain but still… nothing.

He said you had the answer. Breathe, goddamn it! Think! What the hell did you see or hear down here that would answer his fucking question. Think DAMN IT!

"Please I… I don't know. The ground?" Jake spit out exasperated.

"Good answer!" Dr. Pain cheered looking to his assistant. "Isn't that a good answer Misery?" He slapped his knee as if overjoyed. "Damn good answer. Unfortunately…" Dr. Pain paused leaning in until his nose touched Jake's own. "Wrong. But damn good try." The doctor sneered nearly grunting out the last word as he cut into Jake's big toe with his shears, stopping half-way through to savor the moment.

"JESUS FUCKING CHRIST!" Jake screamed.

The pain was immeasurable even by the standards already set in this hell. It shot like white lightning up his leg straight to his testicles where it seemed to explode in a ball of fire. Dr. Pain soaked in the anguish writing itself on Jake's face then finished the cut. Jake's eyes bulged as if a nuclear bomb had detonated inside his skull. The adrenaline kept him conscious to experience every terrifying second. White spots danced across his vision, making him feel faint in spite of the adrenaline.

Smack!

Sensing Jake slipping away, Misery snapped him back to the land of the living. It worked. The white spots disappeared, though Jake still felt intoxicated from sensory overload. His mind cleared slightly, but the answer still didn't come to him. The snip and burn question pattern repeated until he was finally facing his last chance. He was one big toe away from ending the game. Given the gravity of the moment, the doctor paused.

"Now my dear, dear Jacob, it appears you are down to your last chance. You've come so far, don't you want to leave here with at least one of your little digits intact? Do you need another clue?" Calmness was back in the doctor's voice, though his joy in mockery was abundantly clear.

"Please, stop. Just kill me already." Completely exhausted, drool spilled from the corner of Jake's mouth as he spoke.

"But you've come so far, Jacob. Stopping now would just be pointless. Now try real hard to think. Would you like another clue? Ok, you saw the answer in this very room. And if you say one more time that my Misery or I are the answer, I'll remove your balls with a dull rusty butter knife, understand?" Dr. Pain's face lit up at the prospect.

What the fuck is he talking about? There's me and them. Nothing more. Think damn it! Lower than the devil? Lower than the devil. Does he really mean me? How am I lower than the devil? Fuck! Last chance.

Jake cleared his throat and gave the only answer he could think of, "Me?" He closed his eyes praying he was right.

"Now that's the best answer you've given yet! Did I hear doubt, though? Tell me, was that a question or your answer?" The doctor stared him straight in the eye, dead serious.

"Yes, that's all I got." Jake held his breath as his eyes drooped and drool rolled down his chin.

The doctor rubbed his chin as if giving the answer serious consideration before leaning in close to Jacob's face again. He stared without saying a word, building hope in Jake's eyes. The doctor finally let out a long, loud sigh squeezing the shears closed with all his might popping the last toe off with great satisfaction.

"Sorry, you answered poorly." The doctor whispered through the anguished screams of his victim.

One last sizzle of burning flesh and the game was over. Jake was covered in a slurry of sweat and blood from head to toe. He slumped as much as possible, lifeless as a sack of potatoes with the doctor staring and waiting for him to recover. Misery was so happy he was humming a little tune to himself as Dr. Pain administered another shot of adrenaline.

Jake was in a fog, unable to even comprehend how much pain he had endured. He rolled his head back to relieve some pressure from the heretic's fork, though he had sunk both ends into himself to the hilt. All he wanted was to black out or die, but the adrenaline wouldn't allow either. The traumatic injuries were overloading his nervous system, making him feel numb as his mind began to wander off into insanity.

The throbbing ebbed and receded in wave after wave as he sat recovering from the game. He was trying to will his body to die when Misery brought him back to his grim reality with a hard smack. It wasn't extraordinarily hard, but it woke every overworked nerve in his battered body. He didn't have the energy to cry out but it did pop his eyes open. Smiles crawled across the faces of his tormentors while all Jake could do was drool on himself.

"Ah, there you are, you drifted away from us for a second there. So, would you like to learn the answer that so painfully eluded you?" Dr. Pain asked his question as if addressing a toddler.

"Go to hell." The words dribbled out like the drool from his slack mouth.

"Hell? Jacob, you should really be thanking me for the preview we're giving you of what awaits you in the next life, if you believe in such things." Dr. Pain winked at him. "So… the answer? You've given so much for it?

I should think you'd want to know, but they do say ignorance is bliss. Do you feel bliss Jacob?"

"Please let me die. I'm listening, just stop hurting me."

"Very well. Misery, please remove the fork so I may look Jacob in the eye. You can remove the iron as well, we won't be needing it again."

Misery removed the heretic's fork from Jake's neck as gently as bull in a china shop and set it back on the table with the other torture tools. The task complete, he took Jake's jaw in his vice grip and shook Jake's head back and forth, violently making sure he remained conscious. The small torment complete, Misery grabbed the cauterizing iron before leaving the room once more. Jake was alone with the doctor once again.

"Now, let's give you a quick check up to see how much more you can take." A tear escaped Jake's eye. "I hope you didn't think it was over. No, Jacob, we're not done yet." The doctor couldn't resist a single opportunity to mock his patient.

Dr. Pain checked Jake's pulse, placed a stethoscope to his heart, and held the back of his hand to Jake's forehead as if actually caring if he had a fever. He let out several "mms" and "ahs" during the mock checkup. After a minute or two, he seemed satisfied that Jacob would hold up, at least for the time being. As the doctor finished, Misery returned carrying a cup of coffee which he handed to the doctor.

"There, I think we're ready to begin now. Would you be so kind as to give me a few moments with our friend, Misery? Perhaps you could start dinner. Thank you." Misery silently turned and left the doctor and Jacob alone again.

"Are you going to kill me now?" Jake asked, hoping for an affirmative response.

"No, not yet Jacob. Now, are you going to shut the

fuck up and listen, or do I have to have my assistant put the ball gag back in your fucking mouth?" The harsh switch from the doctor's former calm shook Jake from his exhausted stupor.

Jake pressed himself as far back in the chair as possible, trying to gain every millimeter of space he could while remaining silent.

"Good. Then I can begin." He shot Jake a self-satisfied grin. "What is lower than the devil? I'm surprised you found it so vexing. Are you really that daft? You sacrificed all those precious digits just so you didn't have to admit it."

"Admit what? I gave myself as an answer! There never was a correct answer, was there?" Pain and frustration removed any fear of reprisal.

"The only thing lower than the devil is the devil's whore, Jacob! I placed the answer right next to you." He pointed to Evangeline's mangled corpse. "Your own little whore right there, and you're telling me it never crossed your mind? You hadn't struck me as a moron but damn, you're thick Jacob!" Dr. Pain smiled at his sarcasm.

"My Evangeline was the answer? She was no whore, and I'm sure as fuck not the devil!" Anger boiled in his veins at the realization that all that pain was for a stupid joke.

"Jacob." The doctor gave him a stern stare. "But of course you're the devil. Why else would you be here in hell?" Seriousness filled the doctor's sinister features, "Well?"

"I'm not the fucking devil! I'm a banker. Nothing more and nothing less, and she was a goddamn angel! Fuck you for what you've done! You're the devil. You and your fucking freak show up there!" Jake nodded to the ceiling with his head.

"That's right, you're just a banker. A banker

worshipping at the shrine of money. Do you remember what the root of all evil is? You make me sick in your three piece tailored suits, Rolexes, and chauffeured rides. If bankers aren't devils, then who in the fuck is?" Jake could only stare dumbfounded as Dr. Pain ranted, "You worship at the altar of money. You suck on it like a baby on its mother's teat. Do you even know what money is? Do you know what it's really worth?"

"You're fucking crazy. You're did all this to me because I'm a banker? You skinned the woman I love for that! It's a fucking job! There's a million more just like me out there asshole. Are you planning on killing all of us?"

The doctor sat for a moment and pondered Jake's words. He put his head in his hands then let out several times. Then he finally lifted his head, looked Jake straight in the eyes, and shook.

"I can't do it. I just can't listen to the devil's bullshit. I think you're done talking." Dr. Pain took a step forward punching Jake in the face, breaking his nose and knocking out a tooth.

While Jake bleed and spit out his tooth the doctor grabbed the ball gag. He didn't bother calling for Misery, choosing to strap the gag on himself. He shoved the ball hard into Jake's mouth breaking another tooth before strapping the leather band so tight it cut into Jake's head.

"There, much better," Dr. Pain said while taking a sip of his coffee as though nothing had just happened. "Now, where were we? Oh yes, money. The most worthless invention of man. Do you know anything aside from how to count what you use to ruin people's lives on a daily basis? The funny thing is your kind never know a damn thing about it. Is all your money worth anything to you down here? Did it come to your rescue? Did it stop me from removing every last one of your fingers and toes? This thing you've built your life on, what did it do for you down here? The thing that drove you, the thing that got you out of bed every morning, did it have one ounce of worth down here? Of course not! What's worse, what you are completely ignorant to, is that it has no value up there either." The doctor pointed straight up pausing before continuing his rant, "What gives your precious money worth, Jacob? Pretty paper and a government stamp? If I take a piece of paper and write a number on it, does it have worth? You would laugh if someone tried to pay you with a scrap of paper, but I ask you Jacob, what is the difference? Do you even know how this money which you covet so dearly is made? I doubt a simpleton like you would."

The doctor took another sip of his coffee, "Well here in the good ol' US of A the Secretary of the Treasury calls up the Federal Reserve, which is just a fancy bank not part of government as most believe, and says 'hey, we need some money'. So, the government prints up some extremely fancy paper they call a Treasury Bond. Call it whatever you want, it's nothing but a fancy IOU. In return, the Fed prints up a bunch of fancy paper of their own with little numbers on it called 'money'. Actually, most of its electronic these days, but you get the point don't you Jacob? Yeah, I know who you do. Well Jacob that is where the problem begins. You see, every one of those bits of fancy paper comes with this special little thing called interest. The Fed doesn't just swap cash for a Treasury Bond; that swap is a loan and as you know well, loans come with interest. When the government pays back, the loan they owe interest on it too. Now that's just a fine fuckin' thing isn't it Jacob? Where does the money come from to pay the interest? Don't think too hard Jacob, it doesn't exist and that's only the start of the problem. Now when that money ends up in a bank, one just like yours Jacob, it gets loaned out, redeposited, and loaned out again and again. Do you know how much additional money that creates Jacob? You should; As you said, it's your fucking job. Go ahead hold up how many fingers you think that is, oh wait… you're plum outta fingers aren't ya Jacob?" The doctor's evil laugh sent a chill up Jake's spine, "Ok, I guess I'll have to do it for you. Nine."

He held up nine of Jacob's severed fingers, "Nine, Jacob. That's the magic number. Every dollar we ask the Fed to print turns into roughly nine as it winds its way through the world. Every penny of it owed plus interest. What a fine system, huh Jacob? It's a system of perpetual debt, in case you haven't figured it out yet. If every loan was paid back, not only would not one penny be left in circulation, but there would still be a massive amount of interest owed. Ain't that a fuckin' hoot Jacob! Real fine system you've got there, Jacob! But it's just a job, right? You're not the devil, right Jacob? It's a system where bankruptcy, despair, and misery are built right in. You and your comrades then look down at the losers that you created. Do you see how much of a hypocrite you are, Jacob? You ruin people's lives for a living with no remorse or punishment. You regret it now though don't you, Jacob? Maybe a little? What is it you do at your church? Your shrine to gold, silver and above all, green. You act like a God picking and choosing who gets foreclosed on and which of your buddies can keep their homes? Are you God, Jacob? My grandmother, god rest her soul, used to tell me that the walls of hell were lined with Catholic priests but they're not, are they Jacob? They just aren't though, there's no room because the walls of hell are lined with bankers, Jacob; bankers just like you. What you've experienced down here is but a fraction of the misery you've caused out there in the world. And for what? So you could buy another suit or another fancy watch, or maybe get your pathetic little pecker sucked? Was it worth it Jacob? Look where it got you and all for little pieces of fancy paper with numbers written on them. Fancy paper, but just paper. Can you see how pathetic it all is now, Jacob? Do you see the evil of it all?" Though worked up in his rant, the doctor seemed genuine for the first time, "For years you went unpunished Jacob, but down here in my world you've been punished one bloody piece at a time. I ruined your life, Jacob, just like you've ruined so many others. Think it was worth it now? Bankers like you enriched yourselves on the backs of hard working men, but that wasn't enough, was it? So you put the women to work too, but even that wasn't enough. So, you invented a more insidious evil: credit cards. But now what Jacob? How are you going to keep the system going, Jacob? At some point the whole system has no choice but to collapse under the weight of all that debt. You do see that, don't you Jacob? But your kind never cared about that. Look around the world Jacob. People are beginning to wake up, slowly, but they are. But not you Mister Vice President, right? Not you and your banker buddies controlling the world from the end of a spread sheet. Bankers like you, Jacob, starting wars and funding both sides, not caring one lick for the lives you destroy along the way. Look at the uprisings all around the world Jacob. They're trying to tell you something.

"Can you hear them, Jacob Falgoust? Can you hear the suffering? The despair? The desperation? The revolution. You're hearing a revolution, Jacob, but you don't care, do you? You're not listening because they're poor. They can be ignored. They're not important because they don't have a room full of your fancy paper. Your kind have used your money to enslave the majority of the world, Jacob. Did your kind never consider that one day we'd wake up to the lies? History showed you what happens to slave masters in the end, Jacob. Meanwhile, you and the rest of the Wall Street scum sit on your mountains of money, but what good is it when it's set on fire Jacob? Will it have worth then? But here we are alone, Jacob, in my dark dirty basement. The revolution could be raging outside these walls but here we are, Jacob, just you and me. Would you say you've atoned for your sins, Jacob? Do you think one can atone for sins such as yours, Jacob? Can you atone for turning the people of the world into wage slaves bereft of hope until they die? Is atonement even possible, Jacob? You know the answer."

Jake sat, shaking his head as the doctor ranted on. "Pray all you want, there is no atonement for that much sin if I gave you a dozen lifetimes but down here, Jacob. Down here, we certainly try to help you. We do the best we can with our meager tools to help you begin to atone for such massive sin."

The doctor shook his head back and forth like a father lecturing a child, "Your little whore was a screamer by the way, did I mention that Jacob?" The doctor abruptly changed course, "Maybe I did, I can't remember now. She really squealed like a pig with Misery inside of her. Just so you know, she didn't scream for you. Neither when our large friend ripped her apart with his lust, nor when I plunged my blade into her peeling back her disgusting whore skin. She never once called out for you, Jacob. I thought you should know that before you die."

Dr. Pain watched the color drain from Jake's face as he relayed that part of his tale, "We're not the devils down here, Jacob, the devil is you. I consider myself a rather gifted exorcist. How am I doing? I've lost count of how many of your kind I've exorcised down here. All of them money worshippers, all of them bankers, though, I must admit a few lawyers may have slipped through too. You've a law degree too, don't ya Jacob?" The doctor raised a knowing eyebrow at Jake before continuing on. "I guess all that's left is to decide how you die. Care for a say in that decision, Jacob? You can just shake your head, yay or nay? No, means I choose Jacob. You might regret that one. Your Evangeline refused to answer and you see how that turned out for her. So, I'll tell ya what I'll do Jacob. I'll give you three options. Choose not to choose, that's fine. I'll do the choosing from the table over there. I suspect you may not appreciate my choice much. Choose quickly though, I'm not known for my patience." Finally the doctor ended his rant, not that it was any relief.

What a fucking psycho! What the fuck was he getting on about? I'm a good person. I've never hurt anyone. Crazy fuck! I'm going to die down here. Fuck Christ! I'm going to die down here! Evangeline is dead and I'm next. FUCK! FUCK! FUCK! Jesus just make it quick. Please, dear God, just make it quick!

After a few seconds Dr. Pain returned from the table with Jake's three options. On a polished, ornate silver tray, Dr. Pain had placed Jake's three options. First, there was a rather large, very rusty knife about a foot long that looked as dull as cardboard. Second, there was an equally dirty, rusty scalpel that didn't look like it could be any sharper than the knife. Last was an old revolver. Jake knew nothing of guns, but he couldn't see how it couldn't be the best option of the three. Jake nodded his head to the gun, choosing his own fate.

"Ah yes, a nice quick bullet is what you desire. Well let's give it a try." The doctor pointed the gun at Jake's head with delight, "Any final words?"

"I'll see you in hell." It was all Jake could think of to say.

"Sorry, Jacob, I hope you suffer in hell a thousandfold what you've suffered here."

Click. Dr. Pain pulled the trigger, but nothing happened. The hammer fell, but there was no bang. There was no flash. Jake's brains weren't splattered against the wall.

Dr. Pain laughed hysterically, "You should see the look on your face." The doctor was delirious, slapping his knee as if he had just heard the funniest joke in the world, "You actually thought I would load this thing? Ha! What a buffoon! Misery! Misery, get your ass back down here!" The door opened almost immediately.

Misery made his way down the steps to his master's side awaiting his next instruction.

"This fool thought he was taking the easy way out with a bullet! Can you believe that, Misery?" The doctor asked.

Misery gave no response merely looking at Jake with a knowing wicked smile that said, "Now, I get to have some fun!" Dr. Pain handed Misery the gun motioning to Jake.

"She chose the scalpel, so you know, thinking her death would come quick too. Quick and easy isn't what we do around here, Jacob. What we do is pain and misery." He shot Jake another smile. "What we do is trample the wicked like you, Jacob. You thought you were going to eat a bullet, but all you're gonna eat down here is your fucking teeth. Misery is going to beat you to fucking death with this gun, but it was your choice. You two have fun, I'm going to warm these old bones by the fire." Dr. Pain turned to leave before adding, "Misery, take your time and clean up when you're done." Dr. Pain shot Jake one last yellow toothed grin then made his exit.

Jacob Falgoust resigned himself to his fate, ready to embrace the cold emptiness of death. He knew he would suffer, but it was the end of it. He smiled as Misery raised the gun over his head holding it by the barrel then striking the first blow.

Misery didn't strike him in the head as Jake expected. Instead, he slammed the butt of the gun into Jake's right knee cap and then the left. Blow by blow, Jake's knees were turned to mush. Misery followed his instructions, as always, to the letter. This was not going to be over quickly, and Jake was not enjoying a single second of it. Misery slammed the gun down over and over with brutal force. Jake could hear his bones shatter one-by-one as Misery beat him relentlessly, saving his head for the final blows — the killing blows.

Misery's first headshot knocked out half Jake's teeth, breaking his jaw in three places. Jake lost consciousness after the second blow caved in the right side of his face. Misery swung mercilessly until his Jacob's head was a bloody, unrecognizable mass.

Finally Finished, Misery stood a moment admiring his handiwork, basking in it like an artist standing back from a finished painting. Jacob Falgoust was no longer a human being. Jacob Falgoust was a grotesque meat sculpture like his lovely Evangeline before him. Misery spit a thick blob of saliva into the cavity that had once been a head a few minutes earlier. He then turned to fetch some garbage bags and a mop.

<u>Epilogue</u>

The sun beat down from the midday sky as the limousine pulled up the block. The reflection of a perfect blue sky mirrored on the meticulously waxed surface as it rolled along 5th Avenue to its destination. Tinted windows reflected shops, bricks, and concrete with funhouse distortion while the limo rolled slowly down the famous street.

A tall chauffer in a white tuxedo exited the driver's seat and walked to the rear door to let it's spoiled rich bitch occupant out. The utmost professional, he held the door in silence not even looking at his passenger as she swung one perfect leg followed by the other out of the door. She reached out a hand for assistance in exiting the vehicle. The chauffer obliged never glancing at her.

The woman stood, straightened her tight black dress, clicking her heels on the sidewalk as she made her way toward the building ahead. She had been in hundreds just like it before. She knew the lobby was sure to be covered in the gaudiest marble imaginable with horrendous art mismatched along walls with some man's name plastered in gold or silver everywhere you looked. Pushing through the ridiculous giant revolving door, she let out a huge sigh of disgust to get it out of her system.

The man she intended to meet, unbeknownst to him, was standing in the lobby staring off into space as if lost in his own thoughts. She approached from behind as she always did. She took a few steps bumping into the elitist scum causing him to drop his briefcase scattering papers all over the floor.

"Oh my God, I'm so sorry. Are you okay? I didn't hurt you, did I?" Her voice was smooth as silk and the man didn't register a single word she had said.

"Uh… It's fine really. I'm fine." He said trying to retrieve his wits along with his briefcase and spilled papers, "I'm Henry Gisler… um… the third, and you are?"

"Hello Henry. My name is Evangeline Shamaya. Pleased to make your acquaintance."

ABOUT YOUR AUTHOR

Feind Gottes [Fee-nd Gotz] is a horror writing, metal loving award winning horror author. Currently Feind has stories published in six anthologies with several more awaiting release. In 2017 Feind placed in the Top Ten in **The Next Great Horror Writer Contest** sponsored by **HorrorAddicts.net** then later won the **2017 Vincent Price Scariest Writer Award** from **Tell-Tale Publishing** with his story *Vacuity* which will be featured in **TTP**'s 2018 horror anthology scheduled for a Halloween release. 2018 will mark a milestone for Feind with the publication of his first solo published work with the unleashing of his novella, Essence Asunder, by **Hellbound Books**. Lastly, Feind won the **Dark Chapter Press Prize 2016** novel writing contest with the first draft of his first novel, *Piece It All Back Together*, which is currently being edited for a Fall 2018 release.

Feind on the Web

Amazon   Feind Gottes

Facebook @FeindGotteshorrorwriter

Twitter   @FeindGottes

Other HellBound Books Titles
Available at: www.hellboundbookspublishing.com

Cold Cocked

Another exemplary bizarro novella from the great and incredibly disturbed minds behind 'Puckered'!

Betty is sexy.
Betty is scarred.
Betty is an outsider.
Betty is a genius…

…But most of all, Betty wants recognition.

Whether it be a controlling mother or ghosts from her past, it feels like she is always trying to please someone. Will she be able to find her own peace, or will the real world catch up to her?

There will be blood.
There will be j**z.
There will be unusual sexual releases.

But most of all, there will be murder…

Puckered

Percy is kinky.
Percy is perverted.
Percy is a loner.
Percy is sneaky…

…But most of all,
Percy wants to be
left alone.

Whether it be a
nagging mother or
something from his
past, it feels like he
is always trying to
escape something.
Will he be able to
find his own peace,
or will the real world
catch up to him?

There will be blood.
There will be s**t.
There will be unusual sexual kinks.
But most of all, there will be murder…

The Waning

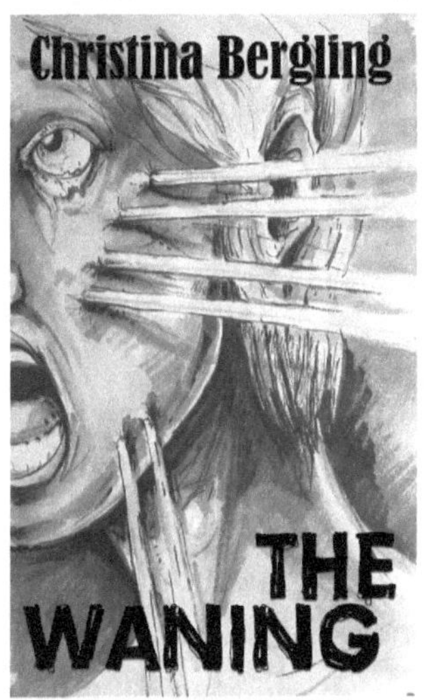

Beatrix woke up in a small metal cage, Lost in the darkness, a persistent dripping sound her only company.

She was celebrating a promotion that was the culmination of her entire ruthless, driven career; a promotion that would cement her status enough for her to take her relationship with her girlfriend out of the lesbian closet; Beatrix had finally made it.

And then she was here, disoriented and petrified in a blackness she could not define. Yet the reality of her Master may be even more terrifying than the crushing darkness and enveloping isolation. He appears as an ominous shadow in the doorway of her cell, never speaking. Instead, he teaches Beatrix the language of pain and torture, of submission and obedience, of domination and possession

With each passing day, the fight and hope in Beatrix begins to shrivel and wane. With each savage beating, her survivalist instincts rise up to overwhelm the person she was. With each dehumanizing condition, she begins to forget who she was and the life from which she was ripped.

Can Beatrix ward off the psychological breakdown of her Master? Can she resist the temptation to survive and thrive through submission? Either Beatrix will succeed at surviving and escaping the torments of her Master or her Master will succeed at breaking her completely and reforming her into his design for a human possession…

Demons, Devils and Denizens of Hell: Vol, 2

The second volume in HellBound Books' outstanding horror anthology fair teems with tales of Hades' finest citizens – both resident and vacationing in our earthly realm…

Compiled by the inimitable P. Mattern and featuring: Savannah Morgan, Andrew MacKay, Jaap Boekestein, James H Longmore, Stephanie Kelley, Ryan Woods, James Nichols, P. Mattern, Marcus Mattern, Gerri R Gray, and legion more…

Shopping List 2: Another Horror Anthology

Once again, HellBound Books brings you an outstanding collection of horror, dark, slippery things, and supernatural terror - all from the very best up and coming minds in the genre.

We have given each and every one of our authors the opportunity to have their shopping lists read by you, the most wonderful reading public, and have the darkest corners of their creative psyche laid bare for all to see...

In all, 21 stories to chill the soul, tingle the spine and keep you awake in the cold, murky hours of the night from: Erin Lee, The Truth Artist, John Barackman, Serena Daniels, M.R. Wallace, Isobel Blackthorn, Alex Laybourne, Jason J. Nugent, Josh Darling, Jovan Jones, Nick Swain, Douglas Ford, Craig Bullock, Craig Bullock, Jeff C. Stevenson, PC3, David F Gray, Sergio Palumbo, Donna Maria McCarthy, David Clark & Megan E. Morales

**A HellBound Books LLC
Publication**

http://www.hellboundbookspublishing.com

Printed in the United States of America